JUST JUMP!

JUST JUMP!

The Double Dutch Club Series

MABEL ELIZABETH SINGLETARY

MOODY PUBLISHERS

CHICAGO

© 2007 by
MABEL ELIZABETH SINGLETARY

Cover Design: Trevell Southhall Design
Cover Image: Punchstock
Inside Design: Ragont Design
Editor: Tanya Harper

Library of Congress Cataloging-in-Publication Data

Singletary, Mabel Elizabeth.
   Just jump / by Mabel Elizabeth Singletary.
      p. cm. — (Double Dutch Club series ; bk. 1)
   Summary: Sixth-grader Nancy Adjei, formerly of Sierra Leone, finds friendship and acceptance at Grover Cleveland Elementary School when she joins the Double Dutch Club, a group of girls who jump rope during recess and, with Nancy's help, earn the right to participate in the state competition.
   ISBN-13: 978-0-8024-2251-4
   ISBN-10: 0-8024-2251-9
   [1. Rope skipping—Fiction. 2. Contests—Fiction. 3. Friendship—Fiction. 4. Faith—Fiction. 5 . Refugees—Fiction. 6. African Americans—New Jersey—Fiction. 7. New Jersey—Fiction. 8. Sierra Leone—Fiction.] I. Title.

PZ7.S61767Jus 2007
[Fic]—dc22

                                              2007012038

1 3 5 7 9 10 8 6 4 2

This book is dedicated to
Charles, Chuck, and Charnelle.
I love you all so very much for the encouragement,
and even more for "believing".

Contents

Chapter One

JUST JUMP IN!

True friendships are like jewels and should be treasured. But not just any jewels. They are like diamonds that can cut through the darkness and illuminate the sky. To obtain them, you must look deep and even be willing to sacrifice, preserve, and care for that which is rare and so often very hard to find."

Eleven-year-old Nancy Adjei listened intently as Mrs. Richards read from the last page of Constance Howell's book *A Song of Friendship*. The best part about being in Mrs. Richards' class was listening to her read stories. Stories that had meaning and that Nancy understood and could relate to. Reading in English was so much harder than speaking it. She had learned to speak the language in her homeland of Freetown, Sierra Leone.

The school she attended there was small, but every student was taught to speak, read, and write in English. Nancy could read, but she did so very slowly, carefully sounding out each and every word. So, hearing her teacher read aloud to the class was a welcomed activity. Listening to interesting stories allowed Nancy to rest in a place that gave her security and peace. No running, no tears, no memories. No longer did she have to be afraid. She had come to America, and everything was different. Now she had a new life and hopes for a good future.

She lived days that were highlighted with stories that had wonderful endings centered around the kind of people she longed to meet. *Maybe,* she thought, *one day I will read as well as Mrs. Richards, and I will read one of these stories on my own.* With her head resting comfortably in the palms of her hands, she nodded yes as Mrs. Richards read those last words.

Nancy knew exactly what the author meant. It was as if this particular story had been written especially for her. Like the main character in the book, making new friends was not easy for Nancy. But it had never been as hard as it was since she came to her new American school. In Sierra Leone, she had lots of friends. Many of them were first, and second, cousins, and even some were third cousins. She was never lonely back home, but her life was full of fear, pain, and poverty. Here in America, she was able to wear nice clothes, and the fear was gone. However, the pain of her former life still held on to her ever so tightly.

Mrs. Richards closed the book only seconds before the start of recess. When the bell rang, everyone quickly filed out onto the playground—everyone except Nancy. She dreaded recess time because she didn't belong to any group. There were the boys who raced around playing tag or joined in a makeshift game of flag football. Then there were the girls who seemed more guarded with their space. One group sat on the grass and talked every day, while some played on the swings and sang songs. But the group that interested Nancy the most were the girls who jumped a rope game called Double Dutch. Oh, how she desired an invitation to join them —even if only for one recess period.

She stood off to the side watching the girls from homeroom 511 taking part in what had become a recess and lunchtime ritual. There was no doubt in Nancy's mind—they were the best jumpers in the school, and they always drew a crowd. Her eyes studied the turning ropes as she thought to herself, *If only I had the courage to jump in*. But how could she do that? She'd never jumped Double Dutch before and hadn't a clue about how to do such fancy rope jumping. Over and over she could hear the words of encouragement coming from a brave place, deeply embedded somewhere inside.

JUST JUMP IN! Her mind commanded. Unfortunately, her feet weren't able to follow the order coming from her brain. There was one thing, however, everyone knew for sure. If you were anybody at Grover Cleveland Elementary School, and especially one of the girls from Mrs. Richards' sixth-grade class, you had to know how to jump Double Dutch. You just had to.

Nancy longed to be bold and courageous enough to walk up and introduce herself, but she couldn't. She had been at the school for more than three weeks and still felt as if she didn't fit in.

Hoping no one saw her, she shielded herself quietly behind a tall oak tree near the blacktop. It was the widest one on the playground, but close enough to the pavement to give an almost perfect view of the daily jumping action. Silently, she counted how many times Tanya Gordon's left foot touched the ground without missing a beat. The moves she made looked impossible. Yet, Nancy witnessed her do them over and over again. And Tanya did them with ease. She had to be one of the best jumpers in the whole school. No one would ever try and challenge that. Tanya was the tallest girl in class and probably the strongest too. She also had to be the meanest girl at Grover Cleveland as well. The "old Tanya" had a reputation for settling disputes on the playground with her fists. If you looked at her the wrong way, it was "on." But one special day after a regular trip to the principal's office, a "new Tanya" emerged. Principal Redshaw was quick to tell Tanya that she needed to find another way to control her anger. At Mrs. Richards' suggestion, he asked her what she liked to do. "Jump Double Dutch," she said.

"Maybe you can show some of the other girls how to jump too," he proposed.

Tanya thought about his suggestion. "Don't have any ropes."

"I'm sure we can find ropes for you. I must tell you, though," he said sternly, "if you're sent to my office again because you've been fighting, the consequences will be severe."

Tanya didn't bother to ask what Principal Redshaw meant by "severe." She didn't want to risk losing those ropes. Since that time almost a year ago, not only had she become one of the best jumpers, but she also had become leader of the group. The "new Tanya" didn't fight and had a new passion, jumping Double Dutch. However, being mean still came very natural to her.

Whenever the girls got together, it was Tanya who would take charge. In fact, she was the one who would make up many of the Double Dutch routines. To Nancy's eye, it was as beautiful as some kind of dance. The rhythms were exact, and the steps were executed ever so smoothly. She was amazed at how Tanya made the whole thing look so easy.

Nancy convinced herself that there had to be something wonderful and mysterious inside those ropes. In a moment, Nancy closed her eyes and imagined herself jumping inside the ropes with the same kind of confidence she'd seen on Tanya's face. Inside the swirling ropes, she could lose herself just like she did when she listened to Mrs. Richards read those great stories. She could let go of the haunting thoughts from her past. Thoughts that followed her everywhere she went. Thoughts that wouldn't let go no matter how hard she tried to escape them. She remembered how her mother, so thin and frail, kept shouting for her to run and not look back. Her weakened voice was like fuel to Nancy. It enabled her to keep going. As long as she could hear her, she knew she could keep running. "God will keep you safe." Those were the last words she ever heard her mother speak. She wondered if that same God who her mother said would keep her safe had come with her to America.

Nancy was so caught up in reflecting that she didn't realize that the ropes had suddenly stopped turning.

"Hey you . . . !" one of the girls called out. "You there standing behind the tree!"

It was Rachel Carter. She rarely jumped Double Dutch herself, but no one could turn like she could. She made turning the ropes look like a work of art. "Wanna turn for a while?"

Nancy turned around to see if anyone else was standing behind her. "Me?"

"Yeah, you wanna turn or not?"

Without thinking, Nancy rushed over and quickly picked up the ends of the ropes. Lindsey Russo stood at the other end still holding the rope ends in her hands. Her expression displayed her amazement. "Quit playing, Rachel. That girl doesn't know anything about turning these ropes. Look at how she's holding them," she said, pointing. "When did we get that desperate?"

In spite of the conversation going on between Rachel and Lindsey, Nancy still couldn't help but feel important. Two of the jumpers were having a disagreement about her. How could she not feel a certain sense of value? But in an instant, she asked herself a very critical question: *What do I do now?* She hadn't been at Grover Cleveland long, but she'd been there long enough to know that the girls who jumped Double Dutch didn't ask just anyone to join them. Maybe they just wanted to get a good laugh at her expense.

Nancy wrapped the ends of the ropes around her hands just the way she'd seen Rachel do it. *Maybe the ground will open up and just swallow me whole,* she thought. Surely that was better than having the other girls see her at what could be her worst moment.

"Wait a minute!" a voice racing toward them yelled. It was Carla Rodriquez, and everyone knew she was the person who had the idea to jump rope during recess in the first place. If Carla didn't want you touching those ropes, you didn't touch them. Nancy had seen her in class. Like Tanya, she wasn't very friendly either. If there were a prize for the moodiest girl in class, Carla would be the winner. There wasn't much you could say to her without running the risk of getting your feelings hurt.

"Who's this?" she demanded, pointing at Nancy.

"She's the new girl in our classroom," Rachel told her.

Nancy kept quiet, although amazed that after almost a month in Mrs. Richards' class, they still considered her to be "the new girl."

"What's she doing with the ropes?" Carla asked.

"We needed somebody to turn for us, and you weren't here. And Ming's not in school today. Besides, we needed another person to help us out."

Nancy wished Ming Li had been there instead of Carla. Ming was nice to everyone, and she always had a smile. She had come to Grover Cleveland three years ago from Beijing, China. In that short time, she had mastered the English language. She too was one of the best jumpers in the group, and she didn't mind telling the others that the art of jumping Double Dutch began in China many years ago. Lindsey had said it was the

Dutch who started it. The other girls didn't really care who had started the game; they were just glad that someone had.

There was an ongoing rivalry between Ming and Tanya. But it was a rivalry that only seemed to make each of them better jumpers. If Ming came up with a new routine, you could bet that Tanya would soon have a new routine to share as well.

"I'm here now!" Carla said, snatching the ropes away from Nancy. "Probably can't turn no way," she grumbled.

Nancy couldn't believe she found the courage to respond. With all the voice she could muster, she yelled, "I can too!"

Why she had even bothered to say anything was a wonder. Every eye on the playground was fixed on her. Even the girls who played on the swings and the group who only sat and talked had come over to see what was going on. Surely they knew if this new girl had the guts to speak up like she did to Carla, she had to know her stuff. Unfortunately, she had played right into Carla's hands.

Carla picked up the ropes and walked back toward Nancy. A peculiar grin covered her entire face. "Well, turn then," she said, handing the ropes back to Nancy.

Nancy slowly began to wrap the ropes around her wrists. First she did the right, and then the left. She'd seen it done so many times. She wanted to at least feel confident about that.

"So here's your big chance!" Carla bellowed.

"She'll do okay," Rachel said. "Go ahead, Nancy—turn the ropes."

Nancy felt a little better knowing that at least one person believed she could do what she said. Silently, she said a prayer. She remembered how the Christian missionaries had taught her mother to pray, and in turn, her mother had shared that teaching with her. They had told her mother of God's great power, and how He had the ability to hear prayers no matter where a person might be. They said if she believed she could experience joy in times when there was none. She could be at peace in any situation. Oh, how Nancy needed this God of her mother and the missionaries to hear her prayers now.

She hadn't even begun to turn, but could feel her palms sweating. Her wrists stiffened as though frozen. Fear had overtaken her. Everyone was laughing and pointing at the girl who wanted so badly to be part of a group that didn't seem to want her. Without looking at anyone, she dropped the ropes and ran back to class. Only seconds later, the bell rang signaling the end of recess. Nancy felt she had missed the opportunity of a lifetime. Not only had she let Rachel down; she felt as if she had let God down as well. Maybe if she had believed a little harder, something special would have happened. All she could do was pray that one day they both might give her another chance.

Chapter Two

The Tutor

TWO weeks passed quickly, and everything was right back where it started. No one said anything to Nancy about joining the group during recess, and she continued to stand behind the tree and watch from afar. Her grades in reading continued to suffer. From where Nancy stood, nothing was getting any better. She felt like she was never going to improve, and maybe now would be a good time to give up.

Mrs. Richards must have sensed the deep frustration Nancy was feeling, because she had an interesting idea. She told Ming and Nancy to sit at a table in the back of the room and take turns reading parts of that day's story to each other. Without any disagreement or delay, Ming stood up with her book in hand and headed for the table. Even though every head was down and the other students appeared totally engaged in the assignment, Nancy could feel every eye in the room watching them. In spite of the scrutiny she felt, Nancy likewise stood up and followed Ming to the table in the back of the room. The girls sat down and opened their books to the selection Mrs. Richards had written on the board.

Nancy didn't want to read first. She was extremely nervous and didn't want to explain. She hoped somehow that Ming would understand.

"You go first," Nancy suggested.

Ming looked at her with her usual cheery smile. "Okay!" She began to read, and Nancy found herself again slipping into that peaceful place she'd created when she listened to Mrs. Richards. She obviously wasn't keeping her place, because when Ming came to a stop at the end of the first page, Nancy was surprised.

"Your turn," Ming said sweetly.

"Oh, yeah," Nancy replied, as she struggled to find her place.

Ming pointed her finger to the top of the next page. "Right here," she said.

"Thank you." Nancy put her finger under the first word on the page and began moving her lips to sound out the words. Not one single word came out of her mouth.

"How about I say the words and you say them after me?" Ming suggested.

Nancy nodded her head yes, saying each word after Ming.

The rest of the class had finished when the girls brought their books up to Mrs. Richards. "Thank you, Ming, for helping Nancy, and thank you, Nancy, for helping Ming. You may take your seats."

What an interesting thing for Mrs. Richards to say, Nancy thought. *She thanked her for helping Ming. How had she done that?* she wondered. Everyone knew Ming was an excellent reader. Nevertheless, it made Nancy feel good to know she may have done something to help someone else, even if she didn't know what it was.

When it was time for recess, as usual, Nancy was the last person to leave the room. As she stepped outside the door, she was surprised to see Ming standing there.

"Do you want to learn to jump?" she asked.

Nancy couldn't believe what she was hearing. Had Ming read her thoughts and seen what was in her heart?

"Yes!" she said. The excitement she felt showed all over her face. "Will you teach me?"

"We'll help each other. Just like the reading."

Again, Nancy didn't know how she was helping the situation, but the offer was too good to pass up. "But what about the others? Will it be okay if I . . ."

"Come on," Ming assured her. "Everything will be okay."

The two of them walked over to where Rachel, Lindsey, Carla, and Tanya were untangling the ropes. "Nancy's going to jump with us today," Ming said boldly.

Carla began to laugh. "Quit playing, girl. She can't jump! She can't even turn!"

"So we will teach her," Ming said with a smile. "Just like I helped you, we will help her."

Suddenly, Nancy realized that the other girls hadn't always been such terrific jumpers. They too at some point had been beginners. They were beginners who had become better over time. And she knew it was true because Carla offered no challenge to what Ming said. In class, Ming was quiet, polite, and always a pleasant girl. However, when it came to recess time, she became a real force to be reckoned with. Though small in size, she appeared to be a tower of strength, and the others respected her words.

"Maybe we can show her how to turn first?" Ming walked to one end of the ropes where Rachel was standing.

"Yeah," said Carla. "If she's gonna jump, she has to learn how to turn first."

"All right, watch me," Rachel said, looking at Nancy. "All you have to do is wrap the ends of the rope around your wrists and hold them in your hands like this. Then turn this hand this way and the other one this way. You see?"

"I think I get it," Nancy said. But she knew Rachel had moved a little too fast for her to understand everything she'd just told her.

When Rachel handed her the ropes, she could see Tanya and Carla looking a bit unhappy. "Can she hurry up?" Carla shouted. "We're not gonna get a chance to jump today."

Lindsey, who was holding the ropes at the other end, shouted back, "Let's at least give her a chance. Just turn like I do, Nancy. This one first," she said, holding up her right arm. "Start with me."

Nancy felt good about hearing an encouraging word from Lindsey. So she wrapped the ropes around her wrists like Rachel had shown her and placed the ends in her hands. With her right hand she began to turn along with Lindsey. Then she did the same with her left. Soon both hands were moving at the same time.

"That's it!" Lindsey yelled. "Just keep it up. You've got it! You've got it!"

While Nancy and Lindsey turned, Carla, Rachel, and Ming jumped in. *What a beautiful sight,* Nancy thought to herself. She silently thanked God. "Yeah," she said excitedly. "I'VE GOT IT!"

For the next several weeks, Ming divided her recess and lunchtime between helping Nancy learn everything she could about Double Dutch and jumping with her friends. She thought it was amazing how Nancy seemed to catch on so fast. Even more interesting was the fact that the better Nancy became at jumping rope, the better her reading became as well. She didn't know what to think or what to make of it. She only knew she was starting to feel real good about coming to Grover Cleveland Elementary School. And even more than that, she was glad she had been placed in Mrs. Richards' class most of all.

Ming was becoming a good friend to Nancy, and now Nancy looked forward to the time when she'd hear Mrs. Richards tell them to take their books to the table in the back and read. Surprisingly, she was even volunteering to read the assigned pages first. Nancy could feel herself not only becoming a jumper who was getting pretty good at Double Dutch; she was becoming a pretty good student as well. However, it took her by surprise just the same when one afternoon Ming, with her kind eyes and smiling face, looked at her and said, "You're ready!"

"Ready for what?" Nancy asked her.

"Ready to jump Double Dutch!"

Nancy asked Ming, "Isn't that what I've been doing?"

Ming could tell that Nancy didn't follow what she was telling her. "No," she said, pointing over to the girls jumping rope on the blacktop. "You're now ready to jump with the rest of us."

In that moment, Nancy could feel her nerves starting to creep up and take control. She vividly remembered that first time when Rachel had asked her to turn for them. She had run away feeling absolutely awful. "You know they don't want me there. I think after you've helped me some more, then maybe . . ."

As though unwilling to accept Nancy's feelings of insecurity, Ming grabbed her by the arm. "C'mon," she said, leading her over to where the girls were jumping rope on the pavement.

"Hi, Ming!" shouted Lindsey. "You jumping today?"

"Yes, and so is Nancy."

Nancy liked the way Ming was so sure of herself. She hadn't asked if Nancy could jump with them today; she just saw fit to include her.

"Here we go again," Carla said.

"Yeah," Tanya echoed. "Here we go again."

"Maybe we should just keep turning," Rachel said. "Go ahead, Nancy. Show us what you've got!"

Nancy looked at Ming, and her smile gave Nancy the confidence that she needed. Ming offered her words of encouragement. "A teacher can only recognize the value of her teaching when she sees her student can keep learning without her."

Nancy was confused by what Ming had just said, but didn't want to let her down. She took the deepest breath possible, braced herself, and walked up to the ropes.

When she got close enough, she let her feet and body move rhythmically back and forth until she saw the perfect opportunity to jump in. She ignored the silence of the other girls and leaped into the ropes. Pretty soon, Tanya jumped in behind her. "Not bad," Tanya said, giving what could only be considered a compliment.

Nancy wasn't completely ready when Tanya gave Lindsey and Rachel a command. "Faster," she shouted.

For only a few seconds Nancy's feet were able to keep up, but soon they both became entangled in the ropes and stopped. She couldn't believe her ears when Tanya looked at her and said, "Tomorrow you turn before you jump."

"No problem," Nancy said. "I will turn." She felt honored that Tanya had unofficially included her as part of the group. She glanced over at Ming and mouthed the words, "Thank you."

"Since you're going to jump with us, I guess you won't mind carrying the ropes inside," Carla said, placing the bundled ropes in Nancy's arms.

Nancy smiled as she, Ming, Carla, Rachel, Tanya, and Lindsey walked together toward the school. *What a great day this has been*, Nancy thought as she stepped inside the building. Nancy believed the God of the missionaries, the God her mother had told her about to be true. He had indeed heard her prayers. And one thing she felt was certain. He too had come to America.

Chapter Three

The Notice

TO Rachel, this day seemed no different from any other. She had crawled out of bed after ignoring her alarm clock for the second time and almost in a zombie-like fashion had managed to get herself up and dressed. She walked the same three blocks to school as she had done every day since third grade. She arrived on time, took her seat, and did what seemed like a morning filled with math problems and tons of reading. Everything was pretty much the same throughout the day. She ate her lunch as fast as she could swallow and then raced out into the schoolyard to meet the other girls for Double Dutch. On this day, the others turned while she jumped. Everything after that was a blur. Everything except what happened on her way home from school.

As she walked by the neighborhood Sunny Mart, something caught her eye. She couldn't believe what she saw. But there it was as big as day. She may have had some difficulty reading that ten-page story earlier that morning, but none of the words in front of her right now presented a challenge. Right there pasted on the front of the Mart window were the following words:

ANNOUNCING: A DOUBLE DUTCH
COMPETITION! ALL JUMPERS
AGES 10–12 ARE INVITED TO PARTICIPATE!

Rachel didn't even stop to read the rest of the details. Just as fast as her feet would carry her, she raced inside the store to find out more about the upcoming competition.

When she went inside, she saw the owner, Mr. A.J., a tall, gray-haired man with horn-rimmed glasses resting on the end of his nose, standing behind the counter. He was reading a newspaper since he didn't have any customers. Funny thing—she had often wondered what people who work in stores do when they have no customers. Rachel waited patiently for him to look up and see her standing there. But he didn't. He continued to turn the pages of the paper he had spread across the counter and never looked up. Rachel coughed as though clearing her throat. *This was sure to get his attention*, she thought. But she had to cough loudly two more times before he would lift his eyes from his paper. She felt her throat getting dry when he finally asked, "May I help you?"

By now, Rachel was so nervous, she found herself searching for the words to come out of her mouth. "Mr. A.J. . . . the . . . the competition . . ."

"Yes, ma'am, that's my name. What competition?"

Somehow having him not understand her question helped Rachel to find the courage and volume to ask again. "The Double Dutch competition," she said, pointing to the sign in the window.

"Oh, that. I really don't know what it's about. A lady came in here yesterday and asked if she could put that sign in the window and leave some flyers in case anybody was interested."

"I'm interested."

"Well, help yourself," he said, pointing at a small stack of papers resting on the far end of the counter.

Immediately, she went to the end of the counter and picked up a flyer. She looked back toward Mr. A.J., who had resumed reading his newspaper. "Can I have more than one?" she asked.

"Take as many as you want."

Holding the first flyer in her hand, she picked up

some more. "One, two, three, four, five. That's enough for everybody," she said out loud. "Thank you!"

"You're quite welcome, young lady."

As Rachel left the Sunny Mart on her way home, she thought to herself, *Jumping Double Dutch will never be the same.*

When Rachel made it home, she ran to her room as fast as her two legs would carry her. She dropped her books and leaped onto her bed, staring at the notice. She must have read it over five times before she said, "Just wait till I tell them about this!" According to the flyer, registration for the event was due in two weeks. And they needed a fifty-dollar registration fee and a sponsor. Rachel didn't know what a sponsor was, but she knew if it had anything to do with her and the other girls getting into the competition, she would find out.

It was still early in the afternoon, but today she felt like getting her homework done. She even wanted to go to bed on time and get a good night's rest. She wanted to dream about winning the Double Dutch competition. Lunchtime couldn't come soon enough for her to tell the others. But then she thought, *What if they don't want to be a part of this whole thing? Then what? Would that be the end of what appeared to be absolutely the best opportunity?* Just as quickly as she had that thought, she erased every bit of it from her mind. "Of course they'll want to be in it," she told herself.

She carefully folded the five flyers and placed them inside one of her books. This way, they would be safe and secure and ready to give out to the other girls tomorrow. But then, she thought, *What will Mom and Dad say about it?*

By the time her mother had come in from work, Rachel had fallen asleep on her bed. Her mother looked into the room to see her covered with a textbook and some papers. She hadn't made it in time to set the table, but the sight of her resting with her textbook next to her made her mother pleased. She walked in and gently kissed Rachel on the forehead, turned around, and quietly closed the door.

An hour passed by before Rachel awakened to the smell of dinner cooking in the kitchen. She hadn't heard either of her parents come in, but now she heard them talking in the next room. Hearing what they were saying was difficult, but she was able to make out that they had received another homework notice from Mrs. Richards.

She knew she could probably convince her mother to let her enter the competition, but getting her father to say yes was surely going to be a challenge. Rachel knew how her dad felt about her taking her schoolwork more seriously, and to Alexander E. Carter, nothing was more important than his daughter's education. Rachel knew she hadn't been doing her best in school, but she decided asking for permission to enter the competition was worth a try anyway.

The first thing she could do, she thought, was to set the table like she should have done earlier. She quickly jumped to her feet and raced to the kitchen, but before leaving her room, she retrieved one of the flyers from her book so that when the time was right, she could show it to her parents.

Rachel really enjoyed helping her mother in the kitchen and was disappointed about falling asleep. Only a few seconds had passed when she turned around and saw her parents standing in the doorway. Her father was holding the note from Mrs. Richards. "Hi, Mom! Hi, Dad!" she said in the cheeriest voice she could muster.

"Well, hello to you too, Rachel," her mother said, "or should I call you Sleeping Beauty?"

She felt a little more at ease by her mother's comment, but worried about the serious look on her father's face. "How are you today?" he asked.

"Fine," she answered softly. Managing a half-smile, Rachel said, "Sorry about not setting the table, but if you want, I'll wash the dishes after dinner . . . okay?"

"I guess that sounds like a good deal to me," her mother agreed.

"Rachel, we need to talk to you," said her father. His tone gave every indication that the topic was something important. She knew what her dad needed to talk about. She'd heard her parents talking, and she could see the letter in his hand. Rachel knew there was only one thing she could do to make it right. "Dad, I'm sorry, and I promise not to miss any more homework."

Her parents looked at each other, not knowing whether to believe their daughter or not. This wasn't the first note they had received regarding missing homework. She could see by the expressions on their faces that they were fed up. And although coming up with a creative excuse or just outright lying had never been a problem, Rachel resolved that telling the truth would be the best thing to do. "I know I've said this before, but I really mean it this time. I will do all of my homework." Before they had a chance to say anything, she raced to her room and brought back all the homework assignments she had done that afternoon. "See!" she said, handing the papers to her father.

"Now, what would be the reason that you would come home today and do all of this homework?"

Rachel's half-smile now turned into a full-fledged grin. "Can I show you this?" she asked, lifting up the flyer she had held back in her hand.

"And what is that?" asked her mother.

Her father stepped closer and looked more relaxed. "Whatever it is, it must be pretty important if it had anything to do with you doing all this homework!" He waited a few seconds.

"You did complete it, right?"

"Yes, I did," she declared proudly.

Mr. Carter sat down at the table. "So what's got you so excited that no one had to force you to do your homework and you did it without any protest?"

"This," she said, holding up the opened notice.

"And what is that?" asked her mother, moving closer so she could see the paper better.

"There's going to be a Double Dutch competition," Rachel said, handing it to her mother.

"Hmmm . . ." her mother said, as she quickly read over the information on the flyer. "Something like this takes a whole lot of practice, you know."

"We jump every day!" Rachel said enthusiastically.

"You and who else?"

"The girls at school. You remember—I told you we jump every day at recess, and we're really good, so is it okay?"

Her father was quick to remind her that participating in a competition wouldn't be easy. "Jumping every day is not the same as putting in serious practice time, you know."

"Then we'll practice a whole lot more. Please, Dad . . . Please, Mom . . . Is it all right?"

Once again, Mr. and Mrs. Carter looked at each other, but neither gave an answer.

"Can we enter the competition?"

Mr. Carter folded his hands, and Rachel knew he was giving some thought to her request. "What do the other girls' parents have to say?"

"I don't know, because I just found out about it on my way home from school. I saw it in the window of the A.J.'s store."

"Who . . . ?" asked her father.

"You know, honey, the owner of Sunny Mart," Mom said to Dad. "All the kids call him and his wife Mr. and Mrs. A.J."

Rachel went on, "I went inside and asked him if I could have one of the flyers, and he said I could take as many as I needed. I want to tell my friends tomorrow, but I knew I had to ask your permission first."

Rachel's mother and father seemed to take a long time before they answered. Mr. Carter looked at his wife and nodded. "I guess it's all right, but only if the other parents say yes as well."

"And," her father added, "if you keep your promise and do all of your homework assignments."

"Oh, I promise to finish everything! You'll see!" Rachel knew she would be held to her promise. She was fully aware of how much getting a good education meant to her parents, especially her dad. He was always telling her how she could grow up to do anything she wanted. *For now,* Rachel thought, *I'll settle for being a girl who's going to jump in the Double Dutch competition.*

Hearing her parents say yes made Rachel feel as if she could jump fifty feet into the air. "Thank you!"

Smiling at his daughter, Mr. Carter asked, "So, do we get a hug?"

Rachel reached out her arms and gave each of them the biggest hug ever.

"I just have one more question, Rachel," her mother said.

"Yes?"

She pointed at the very bottom of the flyer. "Where are you going to get a sponsor?"

There was that word again. Rachel remembered seeing it earlier on the flyer.

"What does a sponsor do?" Rachel asked.

"A sponsor is someone who will back your team financially. They might provide team uniforms and maybe even be willing to pay any travel expenses if you have them."

"Getting a sponsor is going to be very important," her father said.

Again Rachel looked at the bottom of the paper and read where it said each team entering the competition had to have a sponsor. She knew finding someone to sponsor the team wasn't going to be easy, but she knew that somewhere in the town of Cranston, New Jersey, there had to be at least one person who would. For now, though, she was feeling too good to let any major or minor details facing them get in the way. She had good news to sleep on, and she couldn't wait until tomorrow to share it with the rest of the girls.

Chapter Four

Good News

Rachel studied the clock on the wall all morning. She had never experienced time moving so slowly in her life. Every now and again, she would reach inside her desk and place her left hand on top of the flyer, as though making sure it hadn't disappeared and that the upcoming competition wasn't a dream. Then she gave a silent sigh of relief when she confirmed for herself that the paper was still there.

She didn't get a whole lot done that morning. She was just too excited to share the good news she'd brought with her to school that day. Rachel had been working on the same writing assignment for most of the morning. When she glanced up at the clock yet again, she realized it was only a few minutes away from recess. She would finally be able to tell the others the great news that made her feel as if she were about to burst.

Unfortunately, the story she was supposed to write so far only contained three sentences, and writing that much had been a struggle. She knew if that was all she had to turn in, she wouldn't be going out for recess. Maybe Mrs. Richards wouldn't look at her paper so closely that she would notice. She did have the option, she told herself, of just putting it facedown on her teacher's desk as she walked out. This way, by the time her incomplete assignment was discovered, Rachel would have had recess and the chance to tell the others about the upcoming Double Dutch event.

When the bell sounded, like the rest of the class, she rose from her seat and began walking toward Mrs. Richards' desk. She knew what she had to do, and she knew what she couldn't do. She had to avoid looking Mrs. Richards in the eye. If she looked her in the eye, she knew she'd have to confess, take her seat, and finish the writing assignment. As she moved closer to the desk, she could feel her hand trembling. All she had to do was put the paper down and keep walking. However, the closer Rachel got to her teacher's desk, the harder it became.

The student in front of her was asking Mrs. Richards a question, and that delayed Rachel's opportunity to pass in her work. Finally, the student's question was answered and Rachel placed her paper facedown right on top of the pile of papers that had quickly accumulated on Mrs. Richards' desk.

Just as she was about to step across the threshold of room 511 and make her exit, she heard a familiar voice requesting her presence.

"Rachel, wait a moment."

It was Mrs. Richards. Apparently, she had turned the paper over and saw there was nothing much written on the other side. Rachel, with the flyers in her hand, turned around and dragged herself back toward Mrs. Richards' desk.

"Yes, Mrs. Richards?" she asked.

"About your assignment . . ."

Rachel knew her recess time was as good as gone. Mrs. Richards never accepted assignments that were only partially done. "Rachel," she said, "I noticed you didn't get much done this morning." She reached inside her top desk drawer and held up an envelope. "And I'm really surprised considering this note from your parents that you gave me this morning."

Rachel could see that the envelope had been opened, and she knew Mrs. Richards was fully aware of the promise she had made to her parents.

"You realize I can't let you go out for recess if your class work isn't finished, don't you?"

"I know," Rachel said reluctantly.

"Please take your seat and continue your assignment."

She reached for the paper Mrs. Richards was handing her and marched back to her seat. She picked up her pencil, pressed it to the paper, and put the flyers back inside her desk. Holding her pencil tightly in her hand, she pressed it to the paper, but no words appeared.

Mrs. Richards knew that Rachel had a hard time expressing her ideas on paper, so she proposed an idea. "Rachel, why don't you write a story about something you'd like to wish for?"

I know, she thought to herself. *I'll write about the Double Dutch competition. That's what I'll do.*

Suddenly, the words began to flow. Rachel watched her pencil smoothly glide across the lines on her paper. Her story was about a group of girls in the sixth grade who entered a citywide Double Dutch competition. She was proud of the story she'd written, especially since the girls in her story managed to win first place and take home a beautiful three-foot trophy. Yes, this had to be the best story Rachel had ever written. Not only that— this was probably the best story ever written in the history of Grover Cleveland Elementary School.

As Rachel signed her name to the bottom of her paper, the bell rang signaling the end of recess. "Man," she said as she watched her classmates return inside and take their seats. "I missed the whole recess period," she grumbled. She looked up and saw Mrs. Richards motioning for her to turn in her paper. She cautiously handed it to her teacher and felt a sigh of relief when she saw a huge smile spread across her face as she read it.

"This is wonderful," she said. "Would you mind reading it to the class?"

Standing in front of the class was difficult enough, but reading an entire story aloud? Rachel knew that would take a whole lot of courage. "Sure," she said softly. She took her paper and positioned herself in front of her teacher's desk. When she looked at her classmates, she noticed Nancy staring at her. With hands folded on her desk and looking directly at Rachel, she appeared eager to hear another story.

Rachel cleared her voice and began. "The title of my story is . . . *The Double Dutch Club.*" She began reading slowly, but when she got to the part about the big, upcoming competition, her voice got stronger and she read with greater enthusiasm. By the time she reached the end, everyone was cheering. She was so pleased with the way her classmates responded. Reading in front of the class wasn't as bad as she thought. She might even consider doing it again sometime. Rachel just hoped she wouldn't have to miss recess again in order for it to happen. For her classmates, they had heard a good story, but Rachel was sharing what she hoped would very soon become reality. A reality that made it a struggle to control her excitement until the end of the school day. She would be relieved when it came. Then she could once and for all tell her good news to the others.

When the end of the day had finally come, Rachel watched the second hand on the clock getting closer to the twelve. She knew when three o'clock came, and the bell sounded—one might think a liftoff of a space shuttle had just taken place. Though she knew how Mrs. Richards felt about passing notes, she convinced herself that this one time it was necessary. First, she passed it to Lindsey, who passed it to Carla, who passed it to Ming, who passed it to Tanya, who surprisingly passed it to Nancy. The note simply said, "Let's all walk home together today."

When Nancy got the note, with the biggest grin she'd probably ever managed, she looked over at Rachel and nodded her head yes. Getting that note was the greatest compliment she had received since coming to Grover Cleveland. She may not have been a good jumper or even a good rope turner, but she knew that Rachel Carter considered her a part of the group. And to Nancy, that meant a whole lot.

As the girls walked home, the level of excitement

grew. "You mean all that stuff you said in class was real?" Tanya asked.

"Every bit of it," Rachel responded confidently.

Carla chimed in, "There's got to be some kind of catch to this."

"Look at what it says," Rachel told her, pointing at the flyer. "If we do what it says on this paper, I believe we can win. No, I know we can win!"

"Don't we need to practice?" Lindsey asked.

"We need to practice more, but that's exactly what we've been doing every day so far this year during recess and lunch," Tanya said. "Rachel's right! We can win this thing!"

Nancy was beginning to take hold of the excitement in the air. Just the possibility that they were actually going to be a part of a real Double Dutch competition was enough to make the joy she felt inside spill over. "Will we need a name?"

"Definitely," answered Rachel. The others nodded their heads and agreed.

"The Jumping Maniacs!" Carla shouted.

"How about the Jump Rope Girls?" Rachel suggested.

Both suggestions were met with silent rejection. Tanya looked over at Nancy.

"You haven't come up with a name. What do you think would be good?"

Everybody waited to hear if Nancy was going to say

anything. She knew Tanya really didn't want her in the group. If she said the wrong thing or suggested something the others thought was stupid, Tanya would surely use it as a way to show that Nancy really wasn't supposed to be with them.

Nancy decided to do what she had learned to do when she didn't know what to do. She prayed. She hoped God would give her an idea—something that would keep her in the group. Though her eyes were wide open, everything inside of her was asking God to give her something good. She needed a name that even Tanya would like. With everyone looking at her, she remembered something from Rachel's story. "The Double Dutch Club?"

"You mean like in my story?" Rachel smiled.

"I thought that was a real cool name for a team," Nancy said softly. "I liked it in the story, and maybe it will help us win."

"She might be right," said Carla. "That is a pretty good name. What do you think, Tanya?"

Tanya stood there with no expression to give away how she felt. She began tapping her foot on the pavement. Anyone who knew Tanya knew that tapping was a sign that she was thinking. Finally, after what seemed like an eternity of her left foot tapping and then her right foot doing the same, she spoke. "I like it too."

"So we all agree," Rachel said. "We'll call ourselves the Double Dutch Club."

All the girls nodded and said yes . . . even Tanya. Nancy smiled, and inwardly thanked God. She knew she had been given special help and felt a little more as if she was becoming a real part of a very special group . . . the Double Dutch Club.

Chapter Five

The Sponsor

It was official. The newly named Double Dutch Club was going to be in their first ever competition in only eight weeks. The only thing standing in their way was the task of finding a sponsor. They knew if they could find a sponsor who would help them pay the registration fee, they were as good as on their way to the big competition in New York City. Rachel knew this was probably going to be the most difficult part of the whole process. First, a fifty-dollar registration fee was required. Second, who might be willing to give them the money? If this was really going to happen, the girls knew they had to move fast. The best place to start, they agreed, was to talk to Mrs. Richards. Surely, they thought, she would have some ideas. After all, as far as they were concerned, she was the best teacher in the entire world. And certainly they all considered her to be the number one teacher at Grover Cleveland Elementary.

The girls decided on this day they would forgo recess and have a talk with Mrs. Richards. When the bell rang, Rachel, Nancy, Tanya, Ming, Carla, and Lindsey remained in their seats. They waited patiently for Mrs. Richards to notice them. She had already begun grading papers, but looked up and instantly knew something important was on the minds of her students. "Is there something I can do for you girls?"

It seemed to take longer than it should have for someone to answer. For the first few seconds, they looked at one another as though hoping someone would take the lead and say something. Rachel decided she would be the one to take the initiative and speak up. "We wanted to show you this." She reached inside of her desk and took out her flyer. By now it appeared to have been folded, opened, and closed countless times.

"Please bring it up to me, Rachel."

When Rachel rose from her seat to give Mrs. Richards the paper, they all got up at the same time. The girls assembled themselves around her as she read the information. Before she had a chance to say a word,

Ming shouted, "We're going to be in it! We're going to jump in the competition!"

"That's wonderful," Mrs. Richards said. "I'm so very proud of you all. I've seen you girls jumping during recess, and you're really good. How can I help?"

Tanya pointed at the bottom of the page. "See, right here . . . It says we need a sponsor."

"We thought maybe you knew somebody who might sponsor us," Rachel added.

"And don't forget," said Lindsey, "we need a sponsor who'll be willing to pay the registration fee for us too."

"That's not going to be easy," said Carla. "Like my grandma tells me every day, money don't grow on trees."

"We could try and earn some of it," said Lindsey.

"How are we supposed to do that?" Tanya challenged. "We don't have jobs, and since we don't have jobs, I guess we don't have the money."

"I believe I heard Lindsey say 'earn it,'" said Mrs. Richards. "Maybe you can come up with some ideas to earn some of the money you need. You can also start thinking about the business owners in the area who might be willing to sponsor you. In the meantime," she said, picking up her purse from beneath her desk, "allow me to make the first donation."

Mrs. Richards took out a five-dollar bill and placed it in Rachel's hand. "See that—things are looking better already."

"Only forty-five more dollars to go," said Lindsey.

"What about Mr. and Mrs. A.J.?" Rachel asked.

"Who?" Mrs. Richards inquired.

"Mrs. Richards, they're the owners of A.J.'s Sunny Mart," Rachel said with a big grin.

"That's where I got the flyers in the first place. Maybe they would be willing to sponsor us."

"Great idea, Rachel. Local businesses are known for sponsoring Little League and other sports that kids are involved in. Maybe Double Dutch can be added to that list," Mrs. Richards said approvingly.

"As Grandfather says, 'One will never know if one never tries,'" said Ming.

"Well," said Carla, "let's do it."

"I'm ready." Tanya said. "Let's go down to Sunny Mart."

Rachel looked as though she was thinking very hard. "When should we do this?"

"I think today would be good," said Lindsey. "It's on the way home, and we're all here. You know what they say about there being power in numbers."

"What's that supposed to mean?" Carla questioned.

"It would be easy for them to say no to one of us, but six of us? That would be a whole lot harder," Lindsey said.

"Lindsey is right," a quiet voice agreed. It was Nancy, and everyone looked surprised. Though she had been jumping with the group for a while now, she still had very little to say. When she spoke, her voice was so quiet, the others usually had to ask her to repeat what she'd said.

Tanya gave Nancy an angry look. "What do you know? You're lucky we even let you jump with us. And you still can't jump right. Soon as we find somebody better, you're out!" It was apparent she had forgotten the help Nancy had given the group when it came to choosing a name. That had been the only time Tanya had shown any approval where Nancy was concerned.

None of the girls understood why Tanya was especially mean to Nancy. No matter what the subject, she would usually find a reason to disagree. Nancy figured if she didn't say much, maybe in time Tanya's opinion of her would change. *Wouldn't it be funny,* she thought, *if one day we became good friends.* Then again, that would be difficult, given the fact that except for jumping with the other girls, Tanya wasn't really friendly toward any of them.

Just as Tanya was about to continue her tirade against Nancy, Ming stepped in front of her. "Are we going to stick together on this, or are we going to argue about who can and who cannot jump? We must stand up as a group. We must look out for each other. Grandfather says . . ."

"Here it comes," said Carla. "Another one of those grandfather sayings."

"Ming," Lindsey said, "How many sayings does your grandfather have?"

"Grandfather has plenty to say because he has lived many years."

"Well, let us have it," Rachel bellowed. "What is the saying this time?"

"Grandfather says when friends pull together, they will have the strength to stand when everything around them is falling."

"Like holding each other up?" asked Rachel.

Ming smiled. "Yes, exactly . . . like holding each other up."

Lindsey and Nancy liked hearing Ming share her grandfather's sayings. Secretly, she believed Carla and Tanya liked them as well, although they would probably never admit it.

"So we will go to see Mr. and Mrs. A.J.?" Ming asked.

The rest of the girls looked a little fearful. Rachel did too, even though she had come up with the idea of asking them. "Come on," she said to the others. "Let's do it."

All of the girls agreed that at the end of the day they should go to Sunny Mart. And the minute the final bell of the day rang, that's exactly what they did. Deep down they knew that saying about sticking together was true. However, Tanya walked alone in back of the others, while Carla, Lindsey, and Rachel walked together. Nancy walked alongside Ming. She always felt comfortable around Ming. She didn't know why, but there was something different about her. She was always so kind, and when Nancy did feel like talking, Ming was always there ready and willing to listen and encourage her. But on this day, she didn't have anything else to say. It felt good knowing that Ming would readily fill the time it took to get there by sharing stories about what life was like when she lived in China. Nancy didn't believe all the details of every story Ming told, but she enjoyed listening to them just the same.

They finally arrived at the store, but they were a bit reluctant to go inside.

"Wait a minute," Carla said. "What are we going to say? Are we all going to ask, or will one of us speak for the Club?"

"Let Ming speak for all of us," suggested Rachel. "She'll know what to say."

"I vote for Ming too!" said Lindsey. "What about you, Tanya?"

"I don't care who does the talking as long as we get what we need."

Ming looked a little unsure. She never had a problem speaking up for herself, but she realized if she didn't say the right words, it could ruin their chance of getting Mr. and Mrs. A.J. to sponsor them.

Nancy gently touched Ming on the arm and spoke

almost in a whisper. "You will do your best, and it will be fine."

Nancy's words of encouragement seemed to give Ming the confidence she needed. "All right, let us go inside. I will speak for the Double Dutch Club."

When the girls entered the store, they could see Mr. A.J. finishing up with a customer. "That's thirty-seven cents, and eight, nine, and ten. Have a great day!"

The girls stood close by waiting for the customer to leave. When she did, they still stood silently. Ming stepped out a foot in front of the girls. "Hello," she said cheerfully.

"Can I help you ladies?" Mr. A.J. offered.

"We would like you . . . We would like you to consider being . . . Maybe you could give some thought to . . ."

Rachel thought that maybe they should ask for Mrs. A.J., but she didn't see her so she figured she probably wasn't there. Rachel could see that Ming was having a hard time, so she decided to help her out.

"Remember me, Mr. A.J.?" Rachel asked.

He looked at her carefully and scratched the top of his head. "Weren't you in here the other day asking about those flyers on the end of the counter? You were interested in finding out about some kind of contest, weren't you?"

Rachel was glad he remembered her. "Yes, that was me."

"You want more flyers?"

She pulled out the flyer she had taken from the counter. "No—we need a sponsor. Can Sunny Mart sponsor us, Mr. A.J.?"

Lindsey stepped close to the counter and pointed at the bottom of the flyer. "It says right here that we need someone to sponsor our team."

"Sponsor you?" he questioned. "Sponsor you in what?"

"The Double Dutch competition," she said.

"I really don't think I can do that," he said.

"Why not?" Carla asked. "We're really good, and we can't be in it if we don't get someone to sponsor us."

Just as it looked as if Mr. A.J. was about to give them a definite no, Mrs. A.J. walked in from a door in the back.

"My, who do we have here?" Mrs. A.J. asked energetically.

"I am Ming, and this is Rachel, Carla, Tanya, Lindsey, and Nancy."

"What can we do for you girls today?"

The girls waited for Ming to answer. "We hoped that Sunny Mart could sponsor us in a Double Dutch competition." Ming reached for the flyer and pointed at the bottom of the page. "See, right here it says: *All entrants must have a sponsor.*"

Mrs. A.J. looked over at Mr. A.J. and smiled. And he

smiled back. It was as if they had a language all their own, because when Mr. A.J. looked at the girls, he now had a special gleam in his eye. "I guess you girls have yourselves a sponsor."

"Will we get shirts with our team name on them?" Rachel asked.

Mr. A.J. looked over again at his wife. This time she winked her eye when she smiled at him. "I guess we can see about getting shirts, but only if you practice hard and promise to do your best."

"Thank you," each one of them said, looking at Mr. and Mrs. A.J. "We thank you very much," said Ming. "We will practice hard, and we will win. You will see."

"Just have fun and enjoy yourselves," Mrs. A.J. said, smiling.

"We will," Carla said.

"Do you have a name for your team?" Mrs. A.J. asked.

"The Double Dutch Club," Rachel answered proudly.

"The Double Dutch Club," she repeated. "I like that, don't you, Papa?"

"Yes, Mama, it's a good name."

As the girls started to leave the store, Nancy looked at Mrs. A.J.'s hands. They appeared aged, yet soft. On one of her fingers she wore a gold band. Nancy smiled because the God of the missionaries and the God of her mother had helped once again. When it seemed certain that the answer was going to be no, God sent in Mrs. A.J. to make it become a yes.

The girls walked home together happy. When Nancy glanced back she saw something rare. It was a smile that had come across Tanya's face, and she wasn't jumping rope. Surely, Nancy thought, she must have been thinking about it. For now, everything was wonderful, but it was clear that now it was time to get down to business.

The girls of the Double Dutch Club had been successful in finding a sponsor; actually, they had found two: Mr. and Mrs. A.J. at Sunny Mart. Now it was time to practice.

Chapter Six

Getting Ready

ONCE Mr. and Mrs. A.J. agreed to sponsor the team, the serious work began. In addition to the usual recess and lunchtime practices, the girls were now meeting two to three times after school and every Saturday. They were determined to get in every single practice session they could before the competition. Ming and Tanya put their heads together and came up with new routines and showed the others. Carla caught on fast, and so did Rachel, but Nancy always seemed to need more time. Even though Lindsey and Nancy were substitute jumpers for the team, Lindsey was able to master the routines just as quickly as the others.

Tanya never seemed to let up when it came to Nancy's turn to jump. "I still think we need to get somebody else," she told the others. It made no difference to her that Nancy was standing there hearing every negative word she said about her. Tanya never held her tongue about anything. Her words could be harsh, so severe that they stung as each word landed directly on Nancy. Nancy wanted nothing more than to feel that her place in the group was just as secure as the others.

"Keep jumping," Ming called from the side as she watched Nancy take her turn.

"Get ready. I'm coming in!" She jumped inside the turning ropes without even a hint of hesitation. Tanya quickly jumped in behind her. Their routine looked flawless. The movement of every arm and leg was perfectly synchronized and rhythmic. Nancy kept her speed and smiled as she inwardly congratulated herself on keeping up with the two best jumpers in the group. She felt free and alive and wished she could jump forever. In her mind, she visualized the others cheering her on at the competition. She saw herself and the girls of the Double Dutch Club standing proudly next to a beautifully sculpted trophy.

Someone must have signaled for the ropes to be turned faster, because without warning, Nancy's position in the ropes became jeopardized. Her vision of victory became short-lived as she felt herself struggling to get free from the ropes.

"See," yelled Tanya, "I told you she'd mess it up. And she's gonna mess us up in the competition. Just wait and see."

Rachel helped Nancy with the ropes and gave her a pat on the shoulder. "I think you're doing pretty good. My dad always says, 'Practice makes perfect.' Just keep practicing."

"I think you're doing good too," Lindsey agreed.

"I do need to practice more," Nancy conceded softly. "I will work harder."

Ming shared with Nancy that smile she had come to rely on. "You are doing so very well. All you have to do is just keep jumping and give your best. No one can ask for more than that."

"I can," said Tanya. "I want to win . . . We all do!"

"Grandfather says winning can take many forms," said Ming.

"I don't know what that means," Tanya said, pointing at Nancy, "and I don't care. If that girl can't keep up, we need to find someone who can before it's too late."

Nancy had trouble looking the other girls in their eyes. She couldn't even look at Ming, whose eyes always shined with kindness. She knew Tanya was right. She was the worst jumper on the team, and if they lost, it would surely be her fault. Letting the others down in something so important was the last thing she wanted to happen. Before Tanya had spoken her last word, Nancy could feel her eyes welling with tears, so she started running. She could hear Ming and Lindsey calling her to come back, but her legs were taking her in one direction—anywhere but there. She just wanted to get away.

"Look what you did!" Carla said to Tanya. "She was tryin' real hard. Couldn't you see that?" Carla showed no fear when it came to confronting the mean things Tanya would sometimes say. Even though at times she could be cruel herself, she felt Tanya had gone too far.

Everyone knew that Nancy was giving more than 100 percent during every practice. In fact, the chance of winning the competition probably meant more to her than to any of the rest. She didn't care about winning the beautiful trophy or any of the special attention that came with it. Being accepted as one of the members of the team was more valuable to her than anything else. For Nancy, being a part of the Double Dutch Club was a wonderful prize all by itself.

"That was wrong!" Carla said. "Nancy works real hard, and I know she wants to win as much as any of us. You need to give her a chance—we all do."

Tanya could see that her behavior toward Nancy had angered everyone. Deep down, even she felt she had gone too far. Maybe somewhere on the inside, she really envied Nancy's spirit to try. She wasn't the best jumper, but she was always quick to encourage everyone else. She even encouraged Tanya. Though she wouldn't admit it, for once Tanya felt bad about hurting someone else's feelings. "I'm going home," she said sternly. "I'll see you at practice tomorrow."

"What about Nancy?" Lindsey asked.

"She'll be here," Tanya fired back. "You wait and see; she'll be here."

When it was time to practice the next day, everyone came but Nancy. The girls continued getting ready for the competition, but each of them knew it wasn't the same without Nancy turning the ropes and cheering them on.

Two more days passed and still Nancy had not returned. Her absence was being felt more and more, and something had to be done. Everyone was so serious during practice time. And with the exception of discussing ways to make their jumping routine better, the girls hardly spoke to one another at all. Just days ago jumping had been the best fun they could imagine. They liked being and working together to become a better team. It was very clear that something had to be done to get things back to the way they were.

By the fourth day's practice, Tanya decided to take matters into her own hands.

She didn't show up for practice either. Instead, she decided to see if she could try and convince Nancy to come back. She knew Nancy lived somewhere over on Drake Avenue, but she didn't know the address. She soon realized that wouldn't be a problem, because as she continued walking, she saw Nancy sitting on the front porch of her aunt's house. It was an extremely awkward moment for Tanya. She didn't know what to say. Neither did Nancy, so when she saw Tanya standing there, she got up and started to go inside.

At that very moment, Tanya called out to her. "We missed you at practice!"

Nancy turned around and spoke softly. "What?"

"We missed you at practice," Tanya repeated.

Nancy turned around and came down the steps. For the first time ever, she looked into Tanya's eyes. And when she did, she recognized something very familiar.

Surprisingly, Tanya's eyes looked as if they too had seen their share of hurt and pain. These were eyes that didn't light up like Ming's, or show enthusiasm like Lindsey's, or have the seriousness she saw in Carla's or the friendliness she saw in Rachel's. No, in Tanya's eyes she saw loneliness and something else she knew all to well. She saw fear. It was peculiar that someone so loud and so strong could be afraid of anything. But Nancy knew that look all too well, and there was no mistaking it. Though Tanya often seemed tough, there was so much more she managed to keep hidden inside. She never really talked about herself and rarely spoke up in class. Again, Nancy recalled the only time she had seen her really happy. It was when she was jumping Double Dutch.

"Really?"

"Huh?" asked Tanya.

"Was I really missed at practice?"

"We missed you every day that you haven't been there."

There was a long pause between the two of them, when suddenly Tanya coughed to clear her throat. "I . . . I . . ."

"It's okay," Nancy said. "I know."

In that moment, Tanya's face glowed with relief. "If we run, we can get back to make the last couple minutes of today's practice!"

Nancy smiled and brought Tanya inside to meet her aunt and to ask permission to go to Double Dutch practice. Her aunt said yes and walked the two girls outside and watched them head for the school's playground.

When the others saw them coming, they stopped the ropes and ran to meet them.

"Now we are a team," Ming said, smiling. "Now we are a team!"

Chapter Seven

Believing . . .

IN the weeks that followed, Tanya wasn't so mean-spirited toward Nancy. In fact, most days after school, she waited for Nancy, and the two of them walked to practice. Still, though, she hadn't been able to understand why Tanya seemed so mad at the world most of the time, and she couldn't help but wonder why. She figured maybe this was the only way Tanya knew how to cover her pain. If there was one thing Nancy was beginning to understand, it was that hurt and pain had a way of visiting everyone. No one was exempt. Not even Tanya Gordon, the toughest girl in school.

By chance one day, Nancy had overheard some of

the kids at school talking about how Tanya's mother had left her when she was five. Suddenly, she could see why this girl with almost penetrating eyes hardly ever smiled. Maybe in the story Tanya was living, there just wasn't anything for her to smile about.

Though she knew all too well the loneliness of not having her own mother with her anymore, Nancy knew death was the only thing that could separate them. For Tanya, things were different. Her mother hadn't died. The kids Nancy heard talking said that her mother just walked away one day and never came back. Everyone who knew Tanya's Grandma Lorraine agreed that if it hadn't been for her, it was anyone's guess where Tanya would have ended up.

Nancy also wondered about that little red cap Tanya always wore pinned to the back of her hair when she jumped. She never wore it in the classroom or to and from school. If she wasn't jumping, she wasn't wearing it. Nancy was pretty sure that little red cap probably had a story all its own. It was as though she believed it to be a guarantee of her success when she entered the ropes. If it fell to the ground, she immediately stopped and put it back on again. It was obvious that this was one possession she had no intention of ever giving up.

Nancy knew if she cared to hold on to this new, fragile friendship, she could never speak of the story she'd heard. She also knew if Tanya ever wanted to talk to her, she would be more than ready to listen. For now, she knew it was important enough to be a friend and to do so without asking a million questions. She remembered how Ming had told her about the Lord, who she proudly called the Son of God. She could easily hear Ming's voice echoing in her head saying, "Those who want *Him* as Savior should come as they are. He does not judge, and His love is unconditional," she would proclaim while brandishing that huge smile.

Nancy had to admit she didn't understand most of what Ming told her about this great and powerful God, but she did get a real good feeling when she listened. She thought to herself as they walked to practice that if she and Tanya could be friends, there truly had to be a God sitting up high in heaven, and surely with no trouble He could see and hear everything. She was also sure of something else. God must have a pretty good sense of humor to have brought her and Tanya together as friends.

As they walked along, Nancy inwardly prayed that this God of awesome strength, ability, and power would one day help Tanya find her mother.

They were first to reach the blacktop, so the two of them started turning the ropes. There was a definite rhythm heard every time the ropes scraped the ground. Since the others hadn't arrived, there was no one there to jump. It didn't matter, and they turned just the same.

"Hey, that's pretty good. Now let's see if you can turn a little faster," Tanya said.

Nancy was determined to keep up as she mimicked each and every turn initiated by Tanya.

"Well, all right! If they give out any awards in this competition for turning, we've got it all wrapped up." Tanya kept turning, but waited for Nancy to respond. "You believe it, don't you?"

"I guess." Nancy did likewise and kept turning; however, she didn't sound very convincing.

"You guess? Don't you know you can't guess when it comes to believing? Believing is real important. That's what my grandma always says." Tanya stopped turning the ropes, and Nancy did the same.

"I tell my grandma all the time that one day I'll see my mom again. Know what she says?"

"I do not know," Nancy said softly.

"She says, 'Keep believing that, honey. Just keep on believing that.'" Tanya waited for a moment. "You think she's right?"

"Yes, I do."

"Good, cause so do I." Tanya carefully removed the red cap from her head and held it in her hands. She handled it with care, as though it were priceless. "This was hers. My grandma made it for my mother when she was a girl about my age. Wearing it makes me feel close to her. I know she's not really here, but it helps."

Nancy nodded because she did understand. She slowly reached into the left pocket of her jeans. Just as carefully as Tanya had held her cap, Nancy now held in her own hands a tiny plastic bag of soil. "I brought this with me when I left my home in Africa. It helps me to make a picture in my mind of my mother. When I get homesick, I open the bag, close my eyes, and I take a deep smell. And for a moment, I pretend I am back in my homeland. For those few short minutes, I feel like I am back in Africa with my mother, singing songs and playing games with my cousins. Yes . . . yes, I believe."

When Nancy looked over at Tanya, she knew she had answered well. She realized something else—something Ming had told her about the God of her faith.

She said He accepts all people. "With Him," Ming said, "there is no reason to pretend. He knows who we are. He even knows the very number of hairs on our heads." And it didn't matter what station in life that person held. Rich or poor, all had the same requirement. She could hear Ming's voice: "Just ask Him to forgive, invite Him into your heart, and it will be so." The forgiveness would be granted, and one would forevermore be a child of the Great King of Kings.

Ming said that no love could compare with the kind of love God so freely gives to anyone who desires it. "It is a love that can give a hug to anyone."

Nancy wasn't certain about what these words meant,

but it sounded as if Ming was saying how important it was to treat all people with kindness. And Ming was careful to practice the words she shared with others. She had been so nice to Nancy the first time they met in Mrs. Richards' class.

If any of the other girls had heard these words, they would say Ming was spending too much time with her grandfather. One thing was true; she was starting to sound more and more like the wisdom he had poured into her.

At least this one thing was becoming clear. Nancy may not have understood why Tanya sometimes acted the way she did, but if she wanted her as a friend, she needed to accept her just the way she was. Nancy wondered if that was the reason Tanya was treating her nicer than she had before. Maybe she was listening more carefully to Ming too. Though she would never, ever admit it, maybe she had stopped judging Nancy and was starting to accept her for the person she was. Nancy decided if all people took the time to recognize the value in others, maybe there would be no reason to fight or to ever engage in wars.

Before long the others arrived, and everyone was ready to jump. "Carla and I are going first!" Ming yelled. Rachel picked up her end of the ropes, and she and Nancy started to turn.

"Let Lindsey jump in once you two get started,"

Tanya suggested. "Then one of you can come out, switch places with Nancy, and let her jump in."

"That sounds like a pretty good routine," Carla shouted, as she began to move her right foot back and forth. "Let's try it!"

Just as Tanya had suggested, once Ming and Carla started jumping, Lindsey jumped in with them. Then Ming jumped out, traded places with Nancy, and Nancy jumped in. The ropes never stopped, and all the girls agreed they had just put together a great routine.

For Nancy, this was a dream coming true. For a second, while jumping, she even chanced closing her eyes and opened them again to make sure she was really awake. Finally, she felt as if she was one of the jumpers on the team. It was good to belong and have the others acknowledge that her contribution to the team was an important one. She was starting to feel like the girls in the club were her sisters. She had never known what it was like to have sisters to talk to and laugh with. But one thing she did know—if she had sisters of her own, they could never be any more special than the girls in the Double Dutch Club.

As they continued to get themselves ready for the citywide competition, with each passing day, they seemed to become even closer. They studied and did homework together, they walked to and from school together, they spent recess time together, and they ate lunch together. In fact, they were starting to become known around school as the "Double Dutch Girls." And they liked it.

On the way home, Nancy thought about what Tanya had said about believing. She remembered how important Tanya had said it was. Her mother must have thought believing was important too. She believed Nancy would be safe even as she was losing her own life. She believed in the God of the missionaries. The God who had all power in heaven and earth. She told Nancy at night before saying prayers how those who had gone to heaven to be with the Lord would someday greet the loved ones they'd left behind. *This was a good thing,* Nancy thought. *It was a wonderful thing,* she told herself. *Maybe she, too, just like Tanya, would one day see her mother again.*

Chapter Eight

Surprise Package

There were only five weeks left until the city-wide Double Dutch competition, and time was flying. The practices continued every day, and everyone was serious and starting to feel good about winning. If one person made a mistake, the others quickly rallied around and helped with the needed corrections. One look at the girls of the Double Dutch Club in motion clearly showed that a tremendous amount of dedication had gone into their routine. There were cheers, smiles, and plenty of high fives to go around. There was no questioning that the daily practices had paid off. They knew they were at least ten times better than when they started. The thought of competing against other teams was no longer intimidating. They knew they were good, and they were ready to show the world.

The girls were extremely grateful to Mr. and Mrs. A.J. for all the support they had given the team. Without them, they knew they couldn't have made it this far. They had paid and mailed the registration fee, and even bought the team new ropes. It felt good to know that they were two of the team's biggest fans. And when they thought there wasn't anything more they could do, they received a call one day summoning them to come to the store. Immediately after school, they raced right over to Sunny Mart. When they got there, they were surprised that Mr. A.J. wasn't reading his paper. In fact, when they came in, he was wearing the biggest smile they'd ever seen.

"C'mon, Mr. A.J. Tell us why you wanted to see us," Rachel said eagerly.

"You girls just hang on a minute and you'll find out."

He called out to Mrs. A.J., and soon she came from the back of the store and stood beside her husband. Just like him, she wore a gigantic smile. The way they were acting made the girls very curious. None of them had figured out why they'd been called, but from the excitement in the air coming from Mr. and Mrs. A.J., they quickly figured out it had to be something good.

"Did you tell them yet, Papa?" she asked, lightly tugging at her husband's sleeve.

"No, not yet."

"What are you waiting for? We shouldn't make these girls wait any longer. I'm sure they want to get to their practice. Remember, the competition is only a few weeks away."

"Five weeks," Carla said, holding up one hand.

"I know, I know," he said. "And that isn't a lot of time left to get ready. We want you to be your best."

Taking his wife by the hand, he said, "I didn't want to say anything until you got here."

"Well, I'm here now," she said, nodding. "Go ahead, Papa. Tell them."

Mr. A.J. went behind the counter and pulled out an enormous cardboard box. He could see the girls were anxious. Rachel could no longer hold her tongue.

"What's that, Mr. A.J.? Are you going to open it up now?"

"I'd say that sounds like a good idea," he said, lifting the box and placing it on the counter.

"Yes, that's a wonderful idea," Mrs. A.J. agreed.

The girls got as close as they could to the counter and, almost without making a sound, circled themselves around to get a good look at the contents inside the huge cardboard box. They stared at it as though it were a delicious meal waiting to be enjoyed on a special holiday. They were the guests, and this peculiar package contained the intended feast.

Mr. A.J. pulled out a little drawer on the side of the counter, reached in, and took out a box cutter. "Okay, ladies. It's the moment you've all been waiting for." Without hesitation, he took the cutter and quickly sliced across the middle seam on the top of the box. "Well, what do we have here?" He drew back the flaps of the box, stuck his hand inside, and pulled out a beautiful purple and gold shirt. On the front in small cursive letters it said, "The Double Dutch Club." On the back, in gold writing, was the name "Tanya."

"Wow!" Tanya exclaimed. "Is that for me?"

"Sure is," Mr. A.J. assured her, as he handed her the shirt.

"Look at it!" Tanya exclaimed, holding it up high for the other girls to see.

"Isn't it beautiful?" asked Mrs. A.J.

Tanya rubbed her hand back and forth over the letters, which spelled out her name.

"It's the prettiest shirt I've ever seen!" Tanya said.

"What about us?" Lindsey pleaded. "What about ours?"

Once again, Mr. A.J. reached down into the box. "Now, did I see a shirt in here with the name 'Carla' on it? I believe I did." He pulled out a shirt and handed it to Carla.

"Thank you," she said, grabbing for it and immediately holding it up to her chest.

"Now I know we're gonna win! We'll be the best-looking Double Dutch team in the whole competition!"

Each time Mr. A.J. put his hand back into the box, he pulled out another shirt and handed it to the girl whose name was written on the back. And every time, the reaction was a joyous one. There were loud squeals and lots of smiles as the group stood looking proudly at their splendid surprise. They were even more astonished when they realized that each shirt also came with a matching pair of shorts trimmed with a gold stripe down each side.

"We thought this would help you feel confident and remind you girls that you're a team," said Mrs. A.J.

"And we don't just want you to do your best; we want you to look your best too," her husband told them. "I'm sure the other teams will have uniforms of some kind, and we don't want our team to be any different."

"Thank you, Mr. and Mrs. A.J.," Lindsey said. "We really do appreciate all you've done for us."

"Thank you," all the girls repeated.

"Mr. and Mrs. A.J.," Carla said, "you know how people say, 'Good things come in small packages'?"

"Yes, we've heard that said from time to time," Mrs. A.J. responded.

"Well, good things sometimes come in *big packages* too!"

"That they do, Carla. That they do," Mrs. A.J. said, beaming.

Chapter Nine

Meet Edith Hughes

The girls were just about ready to leave when Mrs. A.J. said, "Hold on—we have just one more surprise for you, and I think I see her coming now."

Who could she be talking about? Rachel wondered. *And why was Mrs. A.J. so anxious for them to meet her surprise guest?*

By chance, as soon as Mrs. A.J. finished her sentence, the door flew open, and in walked a tall woman with salt-and-pepper hair, which she wore pulled back and tied neatly into a small bun. Her dark brown eyes sat comfortably framed behind a pair of wire-rimmed eyeglasses. Without hesitation, she went directly over to where everyone was standing and positioned herself right next to Mrs. A.J. She clearly towered above everyone in the room. Beneath her right arm, she tightly held a very thick and clearly worn book. She quickly scanned the faces of the girls. "I take it these are the girls you told me about?"

"Yes, they are," said Mrs. A.J. "And I believe they're ready for you!"

"We'll have to see about that. I'm here to work, and I consider this to be serious business." She looked each one of them squarely in the eyes. "And I hope they do too!"

"Girls," Mrs. A.J. said, "I'd like you to meet Mrs. Edith Hughes. She has graciously consented to be your coach!"

"What kind of coach can she be?" Tanya whispered. "She looks like she can barely walk." She snickered, nudging Rachel.

"We don't need no coach," Carla proclaimed boldly. "We've practiced every day, and we're as ready as we're ever gonna be."

"But maybe she can help us to be better," Nancy suggested. "If she's willing, then . . . "

Tanya leaned in close to the others so that Mrs. Hughes wouldn't be able to hear. "How much better can we get? Nobody can beat us. I mean, look at her. Do you think she can jump now—or ever could?"

"I still think if she is willing to help us, we should let her," said Nancy.

"Look," said Carla. "We don't have the time to find out. We need to put all our time into making sure our routine is the best it can be."

The girls looked at Mrs. Hughes and looked at one another. Even Ming, who was always optimistic, found herself feeling a little skeptical.

Tanya signaled for them to move in even closer. They put themselves in a huddle and kept their voices low. "I say we tell her 'no thank you' and be on our way. She can't do anything for us."

"How do we know that?" Ming asked.

"Easy," Tanya fired back. "Just look at her."

"She may not look like she can do much, but what about all those other teams we're gonna have to jump against? I bet they all have coaches. And in case you haven't noticed, we don't," Rachel said sarcastically.

"I bet they do too. And we need to remember something very important," Lindsey added. "We've never jumped against anybody else."

Carla pouted. "I'm with Tanya! We're the best, and we know it. Ain't nothin' no coach can do for us. Does everybody agree?" She studied each face carefully. "What about you, Lindsey?"

Lindsey hated being put on the spot. And she really didn't like it when the group couldn't agree.

"Well, what do you think about us needing a coach?" Tanya demanded.

"I . . . I . . . think we should make use of every opportunity that comes our way."

"What in the world does that mean?" Tanya asked.

"It means," Ming said, putting herself physically between Tanya and Lindsey, "if someone wants to help us, we should be willing to accept that help. Grandfather says, 'One should never be closed to the great possibilities new friendships can bring.'"

"Do you always have to tell us what your grandfather says about everything?"

Tanya asked. "We wanna know what you think!"

"That's easy," Ming said. "I say yes."

Seeing Ming stand up for what she believed made it easier for the others to do the same. That was one thing Nancy truly admired about her; she didn't seem to fear anything or anyone.

Lindsey added, "And I say yes."

"Me too," said Nancy. "There is always something to be learned. And I believe we will learn something good. Tanya, just as you and Ming have helped me learn to jump, maybe Mrs. Hughes can help us all."

"I don't know," Tanya fired back.

"I don't know either," said Carla. "I mean, what could she possibly teach us?"

Though Ming, Nancy, Lindsey, and Rachel were

receptive to the idea, it was hard for any of the girls to imagine this woman knowing anything about a fast-moving jump rope game like Double Dutch.

"Well," said Mrs. Hughes, "it's obvious I am not needed here." She turned and started walking toward the door.

"Wait!" Mr. A.J. said. "How about giving the girls another chance? I believe they will greatly benefit from your expertise."

Seeing the puzzled look on the girls' faces, Mrs. Hughes turned around and walked back again to where everyone was standing. She gently placed the book she held so protectively on the counter. "Maybe you girls might want to take a look at this," she said. Taking a step back, she winked confidently at Mr. and Mrs. A.J.

Ming opened the book, while the others gathered closely next to her. "Wow!" she said, as she read the pages of headlines. There were numerous pictures. Though the color had faded on some of the older photographs, they told the same story as the more recent ones. Throughout her life, Edith Hughes had unmistakably been committed to the sport of Double Dutch. The whole team was extremely interested in the pictures of a young girl who, at the time they were taken, appeared to be about nine or ten. In every photo, she was jumping rope. But more than that, she was jumping Double Dutch. The photograph that seemed to fascinate them the most was the one that showed her standing next to a huge trophy with a group of girls who looked about the same age. In another picture there were four young girls and a woman proudly standing beside them.

"Is that you?" Tanya asked, pointing at the woman in the photo.

"Yes, that's me."

"And here too?" she asked, pointing at the other photograph.

"Yes, it is."

"You were good, weren't you?"

"Some might say that I was."

Ming continued turning pages. Article after article sang the praises of a young jumper and later a Double Dutch coach named Edith Hughes. Whether local, state, national, or world titles, she had been a winner of them all. One only had to look at the many pictures and headlines to see that many teams had benefited from her coaching. She may not have been very impressive when she walked through the door, but the contents of the book she carried told their own very unique story. In a way she was just like Tanya, Rachel, Ming, Lindsey, Carla, and Nancy. She had once been a young girl who loved Double Dutch and had dreams of jumping in a competition. She had seen her dreams come true and along the way had become a woman who was considered one of the greatest Double Dutch coaches of all time. And in the old, worn scrapbook she carried, she had a most extraordinary story to prove it.

"Uhh . . . Mrs. Hughes?" It was Tanya. Her tone had softened and was apologetic. "Maybe you can help us get ready for the competition?"

"Please . . . ?" Carla pleaded.

Mrs. Hughes looked over at Mr. and Mrs. A.J. "I think it depends on how the others feel. When you are a team, you must think like a team. Even though you are individuals," she said, putting up her right hand with her fingers spread apart. "When you are a team, you must think as one." As she spoke, she closed her fingers tightly together and formed her hand into a fist. "I can't help you if only two of you want my help. I need to know that *you all want it.*"

What an interesting thing for Mrs. Hughes to say, Nancy thought. Though a bit confusing, somewhere in the back of her mind it kind of made sense. She had connected the girls to a goal and a purpose, while at the same time teaching them their first lesson—the importance of thinking like a team.

"We all *do* want your help!" Nancy shouted.

Surprised, everyone looked at Nancy. This was one of those rare occasions when she raised her voice. There was to be no mistake. She wanted them all to know that this was something she wanted very much. And she wasn't the only one.

"Please, Mrs. Hughes?" asked Lindsey. "We really do need you."

"We would be honored if you would help us," Ming said, bowing in a gesture of the highest respect.

"I say we put it to a vote," said Rachel. "If you want Mrs. Hughes to be our coach, raise your hand."

Instantly, every girl raised her hand high. Tanya and Carla raised both hands.

"Well, Mrs. Hughes," said Mr. A.J., "I'd say it was unanimous. I think you've got yourself a team to coach."

"I'd say you're right." Mrs. Hughes nodded as she smiled.

The girls started jumping up and down. They were glad that Mrs. Hughes had agreed to coach them for the competition.

There was still much to do and not a lot of time left. The girls of the Double Dutch Club knew it was now or never. The time had come to get ready for the competition.

Nancy smiled and whispered to God, "Thank You."

Chapter Ten

Let's Get Ready!

There was no question about it. Coach Hughes was tough. When it came to Double Dutch, she was even more serious than Tanya, and that was hard to achieve. If she said she wanted everyone at practice on time, she meant it. She had to be one of the most punctual people on the planet. "Just once," Rachel said, "I wish she'd show up late. Then I'd know she wasn't perfect."

"Mrs. Hughes ain't perfect," countered Carla. "She's what you call prompt! And she probably can't help it."

"What do you mean, she can't help it?"

"People like her have anxiety attacks if they show up even a minute late for anything. I'm telling you, she really can't help it. I bet she was born that way."

"You're probably right," Rachel said. "My dad always tells me how important it is to be on time. He says it'll help me a lot when I'm older."

"You think he's right?" Carla questioned.

"I don't know, but one time my mom went to a big department store and got there before they opened, and—"

"So? That ain't no big deal," Carla chimed in.

"You didn't let me finish. When they opened the doors and she stepped inside, a whole lotta alarms and stuff went off, and a man came and gave my mom a check for one thousand dollars. They said she was that store's millionth customer! My dad said that was one time that my mother's trip to the mall paid off."

"Wow!" Carla exclaimed. "If she hadn't got there when she did . . . "

"That's right. She wouldn't have gotten that check."

Carla shook her head. "I guess it does pay to try and be on time."

Rachel shook her head too. "Yeah, I guess it does."

Practices were scheduled directly after the last bell every day after school. The time was 2:59 p.m., and it was certain that Mrs. Hughes would drive up at exactly 3:00. It was only Wednesday, and today's practice started the same way they had begun on Monday and Tuesday. First, she ordered the girls to stand in a straight line one arm's distance apart. "Now I want you to rock on your heels. Look straight ahead and keep your balance. Don't lean back too far, and don't lean forward too far!" You could hear her commands echoing over the entire school yard, though it really didn't matter. Everyone except the girls had gone home for the day. They had agreed that every Monday through Friday from 3:00 to 5:00, the blacktop area belonged solely to Coach Hughes and her six young charges.

"What's doing this stuff got to do with jumping rope?" Tanya complained. "It's stupid."

When the girls weren't rocking on their heels, they were jogging around the school yard or doing jumping jacks and sit-ups. Coach Hughes even had them doing something she called "shadowing." Each girl had to follow the exact footsteps and actions of the person in front of her. If someone made a mistake, everyone had to start from the beginning again. And on this day, they were making a lot of mistakes.

"What a waste of time," Tanya mumbled under her breath. She hadn't been very happy since Coach Hughes began working with the team. She was starting to regret asking her to help them. She hadn't bargained for giving up her position as the unofficial leader of the group. So what if Coach Hughes had a book full of pictures and trophies at home stacked to the ceiling? Tanya knew she too was a skilled jumper and dared anyone to challenge that.

Mrs. Hughes paced in front of the line as the girls followed her directive. Tanya hoped she hadn't heard her, but she had. "Everyone stop!" Her eyes gave a piercing stare, and Tanya knew she was in trouble. Right away she attempted to come up with an adequate excuse for making the remark. She knew she was wrong and attempted to take responsibility for what she'd said. Slowly, she stepped out of line because she didn't want any of their practice time wasted on the wrong person getting blamed. "I'm sorry." She stepped back into place and hoped she hadn't messed everything up for the team.

Mrs. Hughes wasn't only looking at Tanya. She looked at everyone. "Is Tanya the only person who feels that what we're doing is a waste of time?" She glanced at her watch and waited for a response. No one attempted to answer the coach's question. "Some of you may be wondering why we keep doing this. Maybe you've even asked yourselves if there's any reason for these exercises and warm-ups day after day. I'll admit, the first time my coach told me to rock on my heels and to run and jump, it didn't make any sense to me either. In fact, I knew she had to be crazy. But guess what I found out later."

"That maybe she really was crazy?" Lindsey asked.

Coach Hughes was surprised that it was Lindsey

who had answered since she was known to avoid taking sides when there was even a hint of any kind of disagreement or conflict.

"I learned that in the end, it all pays off. The benefits will greatly outweigh all the muscle pain and tiredness you'll feel when practice is over."

Carla leaned in close to Lindsey. "That coach she was talking about wasn't the only one who might have been a little strange, if you know what I mean."

"That lady's gonna kill us," Tanya told Rachel.

"Girls," said Coach Hughes. "It's all right to question things you don't understand, but it's just as important to listen to the person who is leading you. I'll answer you, but I need you to do what I say in spite of your questions. When you follow my lead, that allows me to be the best coach I can be for you. And it also allows you to be the best team you can possibly be." Coach Hughes waited for a few seconds and then asked the team loudly, "So do you plan to be ready in time for the competition?"

"Yes, Coach Hughes!" yelled Nancy. "I do plan to be ready!"

The surprised girls looked at Nancy and laughed. They couldn't believe such a clamorous sound had come from the quietest person on the team.

Coach Hughes was pleased. "And do the rest of you feel the same way?"

One at a time, each girl raised her hand and said yes.

"Then step number one is listening to your coach. And in case anyone has forgotten, that's me. You'll have to trust that I know what you need in order to make you into the team you want to be." Mrs. Hughes reached for the whistle she wore around her neck, puffed up her cheeks, and gave it a big blow. "Okay, girls, back to rocking on those heels and toes!"

"Not again," Tanya complained. "Can't we do something else? Why can't we jump? That is what we came here to do."

"Tanya's right," Carla chimed in. "The competition is about jumping Double Dutch. It's not about this kinda stuff."

Coach Hughes shook her head. It was obvious that her words had fallen on a couple of deaf ears. She was disappointed that Tanya and Carla didn't understand what she'd just explained to them.

Just at that moment, Nancy lost her balance and was about to fall. Rachel and Ming tried to catch her before she fell to the ground. They were unable to hold her up, and the three of them fell down together. Immediately, Lindsey, Carla, and Tanya came to their aid and helped them up.

"Very good," Mrs. Hughes said with a smile. "Now that's what I consider thinking like a team."

Lindsey said, "All we did was try and help Nancy, Rachel, and Ming."

"Yes, but you stopped what you were doing to help your teammates who had fallen. You didn't put yourselves first. You saw someone in need and quickly did what you could to help. I need you all to understand something. It's wonderful to win, but learning to work together as a team is what makes the winning worthwhile. And I hope there will come a time when you'll even think it's better because you'll know you've already won before the contest begins."

Mrs. Hughes was a wise coach indeed. She had been waiting and looking for something that was different about these girls. She wanted to see some kind of sign that set them apart and made them unique. She believed she'd just witnessed the spark she'd been hoping for. The lessons she shared with the girls were more than tips and tricks about jumping rope. They were life lessons about getting along with one another and the joy that can be found in working together. She knew that the girls of the Double Dutch Club could hold on to these lessons for the rest of their lives.

The girls couldn't help but laugh at themselves. They were learning about caring. They were learning about friendship, and they were having fun doing it.

"Well, now," Mrs. Hughes said, "are we ready to get back to work?"

"Yes, we're ready," answered Rachel. The rest of the girls nodded their heads in agreement.

"And how about you, Tanya?"

"I'm ready, Coach Hughes."

"Good, then let's prepare ourselves for that competition! All right, let me see you rock on those heels!"

In an instant, the girls arranged themselves in a straight line at arm's length. At the sound of Coach Hughes' whistle, they began to rock back and forth in unison.

The next day, the girls were in for a big surprise. Coach Hughes told them to gather around because today was the day they were going to learn some new jumping combinations. She used terms like *freestyle* and *fusion* when referring to styles of jumping Double Dutch. None of the girls knew the terms, but they were sure they were about to find out not only what they meant, but how to jump them as well.

"All right!" Tanya shouted. "This is what we've been waiting for!"

"Nancy," Coach Hughes called out, "I want you to learn the jumping routine too. In fact, let's have you and Lindsey go first."

"But she turns the ropes," countered Carla. "Me, Tanya, Ming, and Lindsey do the jumping. Rachel and Nancy do the turning."

"Yes, and I do the coaching. Nancy, Lindsey, let's go!"

"Coach Hughes," Nancy said softly, "they are right. I have not been jumping as long as any of them, but I am very good at turning."

"How about letting me make that decision? Rachel, Ming, each of you take an end and start turning. I think every person on the team should be just as good as the other, whether you're jumping inside the ropes or turning them."

Rachel and Ming took the ends and began to turn. Nancy and Lindsey took their stance, watched the ropes, and waited for their opportunity to jump in. First Lindsey leaped inside, and Nancy quickly followed. They faced each other and wore great big smiles as they jumped. Each girl's foot touched the ground at exactly the same moment, so they were shocked to hear the blare of Coach Hughes' whistle signaling for them to stop.

"Did we do something wrong?" Nancy asked Lindsey.

"I thought we were doing great. Maybe it was the way Ming and Rachel were turning."

"The turning was just as it was supposed to be," said Ming. "We didn't make any mistakes."

"So why did I stop you?" asked Coach Hughes.

The girls looked at one another, but no one had an answer to her question. But then Tanya raised her hand to speak. "They weren't together."

"Yes, we were," said Lindsey. "Didn't you watch our

feet? We were together on every step."

"Tanya's right," Coach Hughes said. At that moment, Tanya gave a confident smile. It made her feel real good to have the coach agree with her. "So tell us, Tanya, what did you see?"

"I saw Lindsey jump into the ropes and then Nancy followed in after her. I think they should have gone in together."

"That's absolutely correct!" said Coach Hughes. "Let's try it again. This time, I want you both to count. When you go in, go in at exactly the same time.

Lindsey and Nancy must have tried to jump into the ropes together at least another eight times, with no success. But on the ninth try, every step was exactly right.

Once their steps were coordinated, then they worked on their arm movements. After the first two girls finished, Tanya and Ming jumped in, and they turned the ropes. Finally, Carla and Rachel did the same. Each girl studied the movements of the other. They knew they were good, but now they were beginning to see themselves getting even better.

Chapter Eleven

Ready or Not,
Here We Come!

The day of the citywide Double Dutch competition had finally arrived. Everyone got up at the crack of dawn for the trip to New York City. Coach Hughes had arranged for Mr. A.J. to drive his van, and Mrs. A.J. came along too. They didn't want to miss the girls in the competition, so they were pleased when their son and his wife volunteered to run the store for them that day.

Even though the coach had reminded the team to bring their uniforms, she asked them again before they got into the van. "Please make sure you have everything you need," she cautioned. "Once we take off, that's it. There'll be no going back. And you must be in uniform in order to compete."

The girls could tell by the seriousness in her voice that she meant every word she said. Quickly, each girl began checking her backpack to make certain none of the items they needed were missing.

"I've got my stuff!" Tanya said, firmly patting her bag. "All of it."

"Me too!" said Lindsey. "I just checked mine, *and* I checked it two times last night to make sure."

"I've got my clothes, but where are the ropes?" Rachel asked. "I can't just turn with any ol' ropes. I have to have ours . . . you know, the real good ones that Mr. and Mrs. A. J. gave us."

"I think I saw Ming put the ropes next to her bag," Carla said confidently.

Looking surprised, Ming, who remained calm, spoke firmly. "I do not have them. I have not seen the ropes, and I do not know where they are. Maybe Nancy knows."

Nancy found it strange that anyone would think she had the ropes. That had never been her responsibility. Securing the ropes had always been the job of the last two people who had turned at practice. Nancy's jumping time usually came toward the end of practice, so she knew they hadn't been in her possession last. "I saw the ropes a few minutes ago on the ground, but I did not touch them. I did not want anything to happen to them."

Tanya began pacing back and forth, and everyone could tell she was nervous. "A lot of good that did," Tanya said. "Because now we don't know where they are, and it's time to go!"

Coach Hughes had heard the whole conversation and until now had said nothing. "Girls, I'm going to suggest that you all relax and enjoy the ride to New York. The ropes were packed in the van earlier, and now it's time for us to go."

They were all relieved to find out that Coach Hughes had put away the ropes, and one by one they boarded the van. Ming stood waiting outside and wouldn't come in.

"C'mon, Ming! Let's go!" Lindsey called.

"You're not getting scared, are you?" asked Carla.

"No," she said. "Grandfather says that God never gives His children a spirit of fear. I am not afraid."

"Uh-oh," Tanya said. "Here comes more of that Ming Li family wisdom."

"I am not afraid either," Nancy said, speaking to Ming from her window seat in the van. "You should come in now. It's time for us to go, and we're ready."

"I'm not. There is something I must do, and I must do it now." At that moment Ming closed her eyes, folded her hands, and bowed her head.

Nancy thought of her mother and remembered how she too would close her eyes and then lift her hands high as if she were reaching into the sky. This she would do, she told her daughter, when she looked and waited for answers from above. Nancy knew her mother believed her God could do anything but fail. And Ming believed the same. They trusted that there existed a great help beyond anything they could see with their eyes, or ever imagine in their minds. Recalling that, Nancy got up, left her seat, and stepped out of the van. With her right hand, she quietly took Ming's left hand and bowed her head as well.

Just as the girls had boarded the van, one by one they each came out and joined their hands together. Coach Hughes and Mr. and Mrs. A.J. joined them as well. Suddenly, a blue compact pulled up and parked directly behind the van. Rachel's eyes lit up even before the car doors opened. Out stepped Mr. and Mrs. Carter, and they too found a place in the small circle that had been formed. Each stood quietly as Ming asked God to keep their team safe as they drove to New York and to help them do their best. When she was done, she said amen, and everyone in the circle repeated the same.

Rachel ran over to give her parents a hug. "You didn't think we'd miss the biggest competition of your life, did you?" her father asked.

She stared at her parents wide-eyed. "You're coming with us?"

"Of course we are," her mother assured her.

"Hey, look at that!" Lindsey yelled. She pointed to a caravan of cars and one huge yellow bus pulling up behind the Carters' car. The girls were amazed at the sight before them.

Inside those cars and that yellow bus were more parents, family, friends, classmates, and teachers; all had come to support six girls from Grover Cleveland Elementary School who called themselves the Double Dutch Club.

"Now are we ready?" Nancy asked, smiling at her friend.

Ming smiled back, and Nancy understood.

"Yes," Coach Hughes agreed. "Now we are ready."

Everyone got back into the van. As Mr. A. J. started the engine, the level of excitement was tremendous, and the joy the girls felt rushed through their veins and filled the atmosphere. They had worked long and hard. As the van pulled off with all the cars and the bus following closely behind, Tanya turned her face to the opened window and yelled to the world, *"READY OR NOT, NEW YORK, HERE WE COME!"*

Chapter Twelve

This Is the Day!

NONE of the girls had ever been to New York City before. Everything appeared larger than life. The buildings were so tall, extending high into the sky. And there were people everywhere you turned. Never had they seen so many people in one place at the same time. The girls were mesmerized as they people watched.

Staring out the windows of the van, nothing but oohs and ahhs could be heard as they feasted on the sights. "Look!" said Nancy. "It is the Statue of Liberty! I saw it on TV when I came to live in America."

"I have seen pictures in books," said Ming. "I am so happy to see it for real. Father, Mother, and Grandfather have told me about the one they call the Grand Lady of the Harbor. And they were right. She truly is a grand sight."

"I don't know what all the fuss is about," said Tanya. "It's just a big ol' green-looking statute sitting in the middle of a bunch of water. What's the big deal?"

"Grandfather says when people come to America and they see the statue they think of the opportunities that await them."

"What kind of opportunities?" Tanya asked.

"For a new and better life than what they left behind in their homelands."

"That ain't true if your family didn't want to come," said Tanya. "My grandma said we were nothing less than kings and queens in our homeland. I think being a king or a queen beats living in a little ol' apartment any day. Maybe if we hadn't come, I would be a princess and my grandma a queen."

Carla turned around and looked at Nancy in the seat behind her. "Were you a princess when you lived in Africa, Nancy?"

Nancy smiled. "No, there was so much war in my country. My mother wanted me to see America. She used to say that one day we would travel far and we would live here and be happy. She said we would be safe and enjoy our days from sunup to sundown." Nancy's voice softened. "I wish she could have come with me to see that it is a better life here."

Ming agreed. "Grandfather says we should work hard to make the way of life good for those who will come after us. Life for him has not been easy, but for me things have been different. It has been good."

"Yes," said Nancy, studying the features of the great statue as they drove by. "It is a better life."

"I still don't know what the big deal is either; it's just a statue," Carla said.

"Freedom," said Nancy. "Here in America I can study and I can learn. I will grow, and I can one day help others the way so many have helped me."

Tanya and Carla turned around in their seats and faced the front. They immediately began talking about something else. Nancy couldn't tell if her answer satisfied them or if they were just plain not interested. She knew her teammates didn't understand what she was talking about. How could they? They knew very little about the life she'd left behind in Africa, and her life now was so very different.

Feeling that her words were enough for now, she leaned forward and pressed her face against her window and continued to stare at the monument until it became a small, green blur that soon disappeared from sight. She wouldn't allow herself to look away. She thought of Sierra Leone, her war-torn homeland, and she thought of the cousins she had left there. She missed them greatly, especially at night when she placed her head gently against the soft pillow on her bed. She prayed for their safety and hoped she would one day see them again. She thought of the air, the soil, and the rich color of blue that draped itself across the top of the earth. Then she closed her eyes and imagined herself waiting for the dawn of a brand-new day being announced by a blazing yellowish orange sun.

During her young life, she had been surrounded by poverty, devastation, pain, and even death. Each had been a formidable foe. Each possessing a power of its own to destroy the hopes and dreams of anyone who sought to obtain something better. For some unknown reason, she had been spared. *Maybe God has something special for me to do in this life,* she thought. If so, a day might come when the Great Creator would reveal His purpose. Sitting erect in her seat, she smiled and silently thanked God that she no longer feared any of the adversaries of her past. Suddenly, the sound of Lindsey's voice screaming brought Nancy's thoughts back to America from across the seas.

"I see it! There it is!" Lindsey had been the first to see the marquee of the famed Apollo Theater, the place where the annual Double Dutch competition was taking place.

"Yes," said Coach Hughes, "that's it all right! I've been here many times, but I don't ever remember feeling as excited about it as I do right now."

"And that's a good kind of excited—right, Coach?" asked Rachel.

"It's the best kind," Coach Hughes reassured her. "You girls have practiced long and hard, and I'm confident you'll do your best. None of us can ask for any more than that."

"Well, I plan to win," said Tanya. "I want us to bring that trophy home."

"We'll just have to see how it goes," said Coach Hughes. "Remember, this *is* your very first competition. There's going to be lots for you to learn, and there will be more contests in the future. Every time you compete, you will learn something new. And you must use what you learn to help you become better jumpers."

"I think we're already the best!" Tanya said.

"Tanya's right," said Carla. "We are the best! My mama says, 'Think you're the best and you'll be the best!' I'm going in there thinking that *we are* the best! Nobody's gonna beat us. You'll see."

"That's the spirit!" Rachel shouted. "You'll see, Coach Hughes. We're gonna be number one!"

Coach Hughes smiled. "To me, you're already number one. Just go out there and give the best of what you have and I—no, we—will be more than pleased."

Hearing those words, the girls realized that this was the first time they witnessed a soft side of Coach Edith

Hughes. It was a different side, but at the same time a nice side. Suddenly, they realized she not only cared a lot about Double Dutch, but she also cared a lot about them.

Tanya tapped Nancy on the arm. "Wow," she said, "it almost sounds as if she likes us."

"I believe she likes us a lot," Nancy whispered. "The way she smiles when we finally get the routines down the way she wants us to—it is like she is in the ropes jumping along with us."

"Yeah," Tanya agreed. "I've noticed it too. It's like when I see the ropes turning; I just want to jump inside." Tanya waited a moment and tapped Nancy again. "I guess it's a good thing Coach Hughes is here with us."

"Yes," said Nancy, "it is a good thing."

It must have taken Mr. A.J. close to an hour to find a place to park the van, and it took the other cars and the bus even longer. Still, no one complained. Everyone was just too excited. Even when the girls had to unload all of their things four long blocks away from the theater, Carla joked about how the running they'd done during their practices was now paying off.

"What if when we get there they say we're too late?" Rachel couldn't hide her nervousness any longer. "What if we came all this way for nothing?"

"Don't worry . . ." Mrs. A.J. assured her, "Coach

Hughes made sure we left early enough to get here with plenty of time to spare."

"Well, girls, here we are." Coach Hughes pointed up at the marquee welcoming all the Double Dutch teams that would compete.

"Wow!" said Tanya. "Look at this!"

The others quickly ran over to where Tanya was standing. Outside there were pictures of all the famous people who had performed at the Apollo Theater. There was something else in the showcase that captured Tanya's attention. It was a picture of last year's Double Dutch competition winners. Tanya pointed. "That's gonna be us!"

"Coach Hughes," called Nancy, "can we go inside?"

"Sure, we can, but I need you all to do something for me first."

The girls looked puzzled. It was clear they had no idea what the coach had in mind.

"Okay," she said, pointing to a place in the center of the sidewalk. "I need you all to line up right here." She began digging inside the large bag she had been carrying over her shoulder since they left the van. It didn't take long to find out what was going on.

After searching through her bag relentlessly, she pulled out a camera. "That's right, right there." She waved her hand and directed each of them to the place she wanted them to stand. Alfred, Janice, I want you over here too. Just stand in back of the girls."

"Alfred?" said Nancy.

"Janice?" said Lindsey.

None of them would have ever guessed that Alfred and Janice were the first names of Coach Hughes' good friends the A.J.s.

Just as Coach Hughes was about to take the picture, she saw the team's family members and supporters approaching. "Okay," she said, waving her hand, "everybody get into the picture. Now smile big on the count of three. One . . . two . . . three! Now we can go inside, and I'll check on the registration."

"Hang on one minute," Mr. Carter said. "We want a picture of you and the team you worked so hard to get ready for this competition."

Coach Hughes obliged, and she and Mr. Carter changed places. Mrs. Carter quickly followed her husband and began advising him on how to take the best picture. "When I count to three, I want you all to say 'Double Dutch'! Ready? *One . . . two . . . three . . .*"

All at once, the girls and Coach Hughes yelled in unison: *"DOUBLE DUTCH!"*

Chapter Thirteen

Look up and Look out!

ONCE inside, Coach Hughes walked in front and headed straight for the gigantic sign that said *Registration*. There was a long table set up in the corridor, and one could see there was already a long line of entrants waiting to sign in. "I need to make sure they have the correct information on our team and let them know we're here."

"Go ahead," said Mrs. A.J. "We'll stay and man the ship until you get back."

"We'll stay too," offered Mr. and Mrs. Carter.

"What's that mean?" Carla asked Lindsey.

"I'm not sure, but I think she just said they're gonna keep their eyes on us while the Coach goes to check on things."

"I shouldn't be very long. We're already registered, but someone over there will be able to tell us where we need to go and what time we'll be competing," Coach Hughes said.

"Yep, you're right!" Carla proclaimed.

"How do you know?" Lindsey asked.

"Cause it makes sense and it sounds good."

"Come this way, girls," Mrs. A.J. said. "Let's look inside and see what all the fuss is about."

The girls followed Mr. and Mrs. A.J. and Rachel's parents to the entrance door of the theater. All of the others who had accompanied them were led inside the auditorium to a special area that had been reserved for family and friends. When the team peeked inside, the sight of the other jumpers immediately captured their attention.

They were amazed at the number of teams they would face in the competition. The vast array of colorful uniforms made the historic auditorium look like a beautiful fluorescent rainbow. The front of the theater was already crowded with eager friends and family members who had traveled from near and far. Many were still arriving and making their way to their seats.

Everyone wanted a seat as close to the stage as possible. It was easy to see that it wasn't going to take long for those prized seats to fill up.

"Hey," Tanya nudged Ming. "You getting scared?"

Ming looked all around at the people starting to make up the audience and the other competitors. "No . . . I'm not scared. Remember . . . no fear . . . no fear." She hesitated for a moment and then asked Tanya the same question. "Are you scared?"

"I don't know. I didn't think it would be this big. I mean, look at all those teams! When we jump on the blacktop at Grover Cleveland, it's just us. The other kids look at us and say we're good. But here, everybody's good. What made me think we could outjump all of them? Maybe we should turn around and go home."

Nancy, who hid her own nervousness very well, tried to reassure Tanya. "We don't know if we can outjump any of the other teams, but just like Coach Hughes said, we have to do the best we can and try."

"I think we have to remember everyone who helped us get here," Rachel added. "Mr. and Mrs. A.J., Mrs. Richards at school, our families, friends, and Coach Hughes. We may not win, but I don't want to let them down. I'm going to give it *everything* I've got."

Carla pointed at all the jumpers in the waiting area. "But what about all these people?" she asked. "They're everywhere! How can we jump and concentrate on our routine when no matter which way we look there's gonna be somebody staring at us?"

"We will look up," said Nancy.

"What are you talking about?" Rachel asked.

"I'm with Rachel," said Tanya. "I don't get what you're talking about. What are we supposed to see if we do that?"

"Remember that last story Mrs. Richards read to us? The main character in the book told her friend who was very shy to 'look up' . . . remember?" Nancy asked.

Tanya looked puzzled. "Yeah, I do, but how can that help us?"

"What did she say she'd find?"

Both Tanya and Rachel shrugged their shoulders because they didn't remember.

"She said when you look up you can see possibilities," Nancy said confidently. "We will see possibilities."

For once, even Ming looked a little unsure. Still, however, she managed to show that smile of hers. "I think we will do fine," she added. "We have worked hard, so we have nothing to be afraid about."

Tanya interrupted, "Yes, we do."

"What?" asked Carla.

"LOSING!" Tanya said, pointing at all the teams positioned around the great auditorium. "I didn't come here to lose. One thing Ming *is* right about is that we've worked too hard to get here. I want us to take home that trophy!"

While Tanya spoke with confidence and determination, her facial expression clearly said she wasn't so sure. She had been the first to show an indication that she might be afraid, and now tried to find an effective way to redeem herself. "I'll be glad when it's our turn," she said, laughing. "Then we'll be able to show 'em what we've got!"

The team knew their chance to do just that was very close at hand. There were teams gathered from all over the country, and one team looked as good as the next. The Double Dutch Club wasn't the only team who had practiced hard to get there. In fact, in their eyes every team looked as determined as they did to take home the coveted trophy for themselves.

"Maybe we too should make time for practice," said Nancy. "Maybe there is something Coach Hughes can tell us that will help us win."

Coach Hughes had just returned from the registration table. "Well, we're in! We just need to find the area where we've been assigned to sit."

Rachel noticed the folded piece of paper in the Coach's hand. "What did they give you, Coach Hughes?"

The rest of the girls moved in closer. They too were curious about the paper Coach Hughes held in her hand. She opened it up and showed them the number printed on the paper. It was twenty-three.

"What does that number mean?" asked Lindsey.

"I know what it means," Carla shouted. "That's when we're gonna jump! Right, Coach Hughes?"

"That's right! We're number twenty-three, and it'll be a little while before you girls jump."

"We should practice," Tanya said, as she began tapping her foot and pinning her red cap to the back of her hair. "We need to practice," she said anxiously.

"Will you believe me if I say you're ready?" asked the coach.

No one answered, and for the first time, Coach Hughes could tell the team seemed unsure of themselves.

"If you won't say it, I will. You are as ready as you need to be. I know how hard you all have worked, and you'll be great! Now, I've registered you girls for the freestyle competition. That's where you're the strongest."

Hearing what the coach said only made Tanya more uneasy. "Freestyle? Do you really think that's our strongest routine? What if we can't remember the moves we've practiced?" Coach Hughes knew she needed to do something to head off what was becoming a real obstacle for the team. She knew that if the girls lost their confidence, it could have a serious effect on their performance. She could sense fear gripping her best jumper, and it wouldn't take long for it to spread to the others. "How do you feel when you jump Double Dutch?"

Lindsey was the first to answer. "I feel good!"

"Great!" Tanya yelled.

"I feel special when I jump," said Nancy.

"Me too!" Ming added.

Coach Hughes looked at Carla. "How about you, Carla?"

Carla looked at her teammates. "Yes, I feel great when I'm jumping. There's nothing like it."

"And when you make a mistake?"

"We start over, and we keep on jumping," said Rachel.

"Then," said Coach Hughes, "when it's your turn to compete, pretend you are on the blacktop. If you make a mistake, start over and keep on jumping. And do something for me."

"What would you have us to do?" asked Nancy.

For the second time Coach Hughes showed them a great big smile. "Have fun while you're jumping! That's the key. Just make sure you have fun."

At hearing the Coach's words, whatever pressure the girls had been feeling, whether real or imagined, disappeared instantly.

Rachel tapped Tanya on the arm. "So, are we gonna look up when we jump or not?"

Tanya grinned with the usual confidence that her teammates expected from her.

"Yeah, we're gonna look up, but those other teams *had better look out!*"

Chapter Fourteen

Make It Count!

Coach Hughes decided to have Nancy and Lindsey turn, while Tanya, Rachel, Ming, and Carla would alternate jumping. The girls had waited more than an hour for their number to be called. And in that time, they were sure they had seen some of the best Double Dutch jumpers in the country and the world. They thought their greatest competitors to be a team that called itself "Jumping Thunder" from the state of North Carolina. They had been the sixteenth team to jump, yet their freestyle performance was unforgettable. Never missing a step, they executed their moves with perfection. The Double Dutch Club knew if they had any chance at all of bringing home that trophy, Jumping Thunder was the team they had to beat. Getting into the finals would give them the opportunity they needed. This wasn't going to be easy, because only the top five teams who scored the highest number of points in the first round would be allowed to jump in the finals.

Everyone knew what they had to do. They had to be better than the best jump they'd ever performed back home at Grover Cleveland.

Finally, the waiting was over. The announcer called loudly, "TEAM NUMBER TWENTY-THREE! THE DOUBLE DUTCH CLUB FROM GROVER CLEVELAND SCHOOL IN NEW JERSEY WILL NOW COMPETE IN THE FREESTYLE JUMP COMPETITION!"

"Wait!" shouted Tanya. Quickly she touched the back of her head to make sure her red cap was securely in place. "Now we're ready!" she said confidently. The time limit for the freestyle performances was three minutes, and although the team had their routine time down exactly, they knew this was going to be the longest three minutes of their lives.

Immediately after the announcing of their team, the girls came out on stage and took their positions. They quickly glanced over at Coach Hughes, who stood off to the side of the curtain. She smiled and gave them a nod of approval. They also looked out into the audience, where they saw Mr. and Mrs. A.J. and a host of family and friends waving and cheering them on. The Carters even held up a huge banner they'd made that read, "Go Double Dutch Club!" Seeing that banner made Rachel and the girls feel great. It was like adding icing to a triple layered cake. They knew it was time to jump.

Tanya gave a signal for their music to begin. She looked at both Nancy and Lindsey and nodded for them to start turning. Nancy made sure she held the ends of the ropes tightly in her hands and kept her eyes on the first two jumpers. Lindsey did the same. Once they began turning, the rhythmic cadence of the ropes could be heard throughout the auditorium as its sound aligned itself with the beat of the music. First, Ming and Carla jumped in, then Rachel. Next, Ming jumped out and Tanya promptly entered and replaced her. All the while, the two remaining jumpers were completely synchronized each time their left or right foot touched the floor of the stage.

To avoid getting nervous, the girls remembered not to look at the faces of the audience. Nancy smiled and looked over at Lindsey. While they kept turning, both looked up. While Tanya jumped with Rachel and Carla, the three of them also looked up as they jumped. Everyone probably thought it was part of their original routine. No one missed a step. Rachel looked over at Ming, who was ready to come back in. They knew the importance of making the transition as smooth as possible. So both girls made sure they counted in their heads just like Coach Hughes had taught them, and like they had practiced on the blacktop. First Ming put her finger up to let Rachel know the count had started. And when they each got to five, Ming was once again inside the ropes and Rachel was out. They could tell the audience was impressed by the way the people cheered and clapped. If they could just keep their momentum going and stay focused, they would be on their way to getting a place in the finals.

The last move, they knew, was going to be the most difficult. Carla would have to come out, leaving Tanya and Ming to jump. Carla looked to Tanya to give her the signal letting her know when she was ready. Again, the count was to five and they both moved at exactly the same time. In an instant, Carla was out and Tanya was in. Tanya and Ming jumped and prepared to perform the one move they knew could capture their team a place in the finals. They turned and faced each other and counted to six this time. By the time they reached the number six, they locked arms and in a flash Tanya flipped Ming over her back. The two of them never missed a step. When Ming landed on her feet, she and Tanya were still jumping. The team's performance was flawless. To end the routine, Rachel and Carla had to reenter the ropes with all four girls jumping and landing on the same foot at the same time. Nancy and Lindsey held their breath and gradually loosened some of the rope around their wrists.

They needed to make sure there was enough rope for all four girls to jump once Carla and Rachel came back in. When the ropes looked right, Ming and Tanya moved up to make room for the two girls to come in. All six girls began to count out loud: "ONE, TWO, THREE, FOUR, FIVE, SIX!" At once all four girls were safely inside the ropes. Nancy and Lindsey smiled as they turned because they knew the team called the Double Dutch Club from New Jersey had done well. One last quick step in the revolving ropes, and then one at a time, each of the four jumpers made her exit. The last to jump out was Tanya, who exited just as the music ended.

The loud applause and cheering from the audience was almost deafening. The girls quickly positioned themselves in a straight line and stood before the panel of judges. They hoped to get a score at least as high as Jumping Thunder. Out of a possible 10 points, they had received a score of 9.8. The girls held their breath as they watched the judges discuss the performance. When the judge who sat at the far right end of the table placed his hands on the card revealing the results, the team moved closer together. The moment he lifted the card off the table and displayed it, all six girls jumped high into the air and screamed. For their freestyle performance, they had received a 9.6. Not only had they made the top five, qualifying them to compete in the final round, but they had a good chance to win the title

"Best of the Show" for the Advanced Freestyle Fusion category of the competition. Here, their jumping routine had to be a mix of Double Dutch and dancing accompanied with music.

The final round of the Freestyle Fusion competition was scheduled for later that afternoon. Coach Hughes was pleased with her team's performance and their score, so she suggested they have lunch and allow themselves to relax. Mr. and Mrs. A.J., still cheering as they approached, agreed, and so did Rachel's parents. Unfortunately, none of the girls wanted to rest or eat.

"That's a great idea!" said Mr. A.J. "This is one Double Dutch team that deserves a terrific lunch!"

"And Mr. A.J. will pay!" his wife added. "It will be a celebration!"

"In that case," Mr. Carter said, "it sounds like a great idea."

"Eat?" asked Tanya. "We can't eat now! We need to practice!"

As unusual as it was, Ming agreed with Tanya. "I believe we will all feel better if we practice for a little while."

Nancy echoed the same. "I think it will not hurt if we make sure our jumping is the best it can be."

Carla was clearly disappointed. "After all that jumping, I'm hungry."

"Don't you want us to win the trophy?" asked Rachel.

"I want us to win, but I want something to eat too."

Lindsey tried to look away from the others, but she knew the question was headed straight in her direction.

Tanya grabbed Carla by the arm. "Let's let Lindsey decide for us."

Carla knew she didn't have a chance. Of all people to ask, it had to be Lindsey. She would never go against the group and vote to have lunch. She detested being put on the spot, especially when it came to making choices that might divide the team. Carla knew that and decided to surrender her position about getting something to eat. "Let's practice," she said. "It can't hurt." She could see from the look on Lindsey's face that she was relieved she didn't have to choose. It was unanimous; the team would practice.

Right away, the girls formed a circle, put their arms around one another, and screamed for joy. "We've got to beat Jumping Thunder!" said Tanya. "We can do it! Let's make this jump count!"

Chapter Fifteen

Best of the Show

The girls really worked hard to make sure they were ready for the afternoon competition. Once they found themselves some space behind the stage, they practiced their routine until almost all of them were satisfied. "One more time," Tanya shouted.

"We should practice the flip one more time."

In frustration, Rachel threw her hands in the air. "C'mon, we're ready. We can't do nothin' else."

"Rachel's right," said Carla. "We've done all we can."

"We want to win Best of the Show, don't we?" Tanya figured they would probably consent to one more run-through of their routine.

"Okay," said Ming. "Nancy, you and Lindsey turn for us, please?"

"This is it; I promise," Tanya conceded. She gave the signal for Nancy and Lindsey to begin turning the ropes. As soon as the ropes began to move, Carla and Rachel stood ready to jump in. They looked at each other and began to count.

"Wait a minute!" Rachel yelled. "I made up a rhyme. Every time I say a line, everybody say 'Yeah' real loud. Okay?"

"Go ahead," said Lindsey. "Say it!"

"Our club's the best!"

"Yeah . . ."

". . . than all the rest!"

"Yeah . . ."

"We'll take our time!"

"Yeah . . ."

"To say this rhyme!"

"Yeah . . ."

"And then you'll know!"

"Yeah . . ."

"We're the Best of the Show!"

"Yeah . . ."

"So watch and see!"

"Yeah . . ."

"How free we'll be!"

"Yeah!"

"The ropes will turn!"

"Yeah . . ."

"And you will learn!"

"Yeah . . ."

"We love so much!"

"Yeah . . ."

"OUR DOUBLE DUTCH!"

"That was real good, but we just need to go over the flip one more time," Tanya said.

Coach Hughes had stood by patiently up to this point, but she could see how tired the girls were. "Tanya, the routine looks great! You don't want to practice so much that everyone will be too tired to jump when the time comes."

Tanya could see that her teammates were tired, but still felt the need to try the flip part of their freestyle routine just once more. "I promise, Coach Hughes—this will be it . . . just one more."

Coach Hughes carefully inspected the facial expressions of the girls. "How do the rest of you feel? Do you need to stop now, or do you want to do the flip one more time?"

Nancy picked up her end of the ropes, and Lindsey did likewise. "We must try if we want the judges to know how very good we are," she said.

"And we are good!" Lindsey echoed.

Carla agreed. "I guess it won't hurt."

"Okay then," said Rachel. "Let's go!"

As soon as Nancy and Lindsey began turning, Tanya jumped in. Like before, she signaled Ming to start the count. By the time Ming got to six, she was already inside. Both girls continued jumping until Tanya started the count for them to do the flip. Just as they'd practiced it before, she and Ming locked arms and prepared to do the most crucial part of the team's routine.

Suddenly, something went awfully wrong. Ming was lying on the floor, holding her right ankle and crying. She had missed her footing after the landing and couldn't balance herself to stay up. Immediately, Coach Hughes, the Carters, and the A.J.s ran over to see what had happened. Coach Hughes knew by the pain she saw etched in Ming's face that she would not be able to jump anymore that day. Mr. A.J. lifted her up and carried her over to the side of the room away from the other jumpers. One of the other coaches who had seen what happened called for a doctor and brought over an ice pack to help stop Ming's ankle from swelling.

"What are we gonna do now?" cried Carla. "Ming's hurt, and we won't be able to finish our routine."

Nancy, with a worried look on her face, asked Coach Hughes, "Will Ming be all right?"

"Yes, but it will take awhile before she can jump again. It looks like she might have a pretty bad sprain."

Nancy volunteered. "May I please jump for her?"

Every one of the girls stood silent as though time itself had stopped. "Nancy? But she doesn't know the routine the way Ming does!" Rachel shouted.

"I'd rather see Nancy try than we not get a chance to compete at all," said Lindsey.

Tanya slowly walked over and stood next to Lindsey. The excitement she had felt just moments earlier was gone. She gave Nancy a reassuring pat on the back. "Me too," she agreed.

"I can turn," offered Carla, "and let Nancy be the third jumper."

Nancy felt good knowing that she had her team's support. Even Rachel changed her mind. "I'm sorry, Nancy. I know you'll do your best."

"Ming has helped me very much with my jumping. You have all taught me well. I believe I can do it."

"We know you can jump," said Carla. "But what about the . . ."

"I believe I can do the flip with Tanya."

Tanya's eyes lit up, because she was hopeful. She didn't know if this new plan would work, but was glad that once again they had a chance to compete.

"Remember," the coach reminded them, "everything now changes to five. You must think five and not six as you jump."

The girls realized that the coach was right. They still had two people to turn, but only three would jump.

They knew they had to work on their count, and there wasn't much time for them to do it.

The afternoon performance time came swiftly. The Double Dutch Club was number five in a group of jumpers that included the top five from the morning competition. Ming, with her ankle taped, sat directly behind the judges' table and gave a "thumbs up" to her teammates.

Jumping Thunder had once again come close to getting an almost perfect score by receiving a 9.8. One team calling themselves Six Steps of Success finished with an overall score of 9.6. Tanya, Rachel, Lindsey, Nancy, and Carla didn't want to settle for anything less than a 9.9. Once again, Tanya gave a signal for the music to start, while Lindsey and Carla began to turn. Rachel jumped in first and was quickly followed by Nancy. The two of them faced each other and then jumped back to back. As soon as they positioned themselves so that they both faced Lindsey's end of the ropes, Tanya entered. The three continued jumping and included synchronized hand motions they had practiced only hours before. Tanya began to count, and Rachel prepared to come out. As soon as she heard Tanya say, "Five!" she jumped out. Tanya and Nancy were left facing each other inside the ropes. Tanya looked at Nancy and put up one finger to start the count. Nancy knew that when Tanya reached five it would be time to do the flip. The team knew if the flip was successful, they would have the score they needed to come in first place and be named "Best of the Show." Everything rested on that flip being done right.

For a second Nancy forgot the first rule she had learned about jumping Double Dutch. "Don't look down at your feet," Ming would tell her. "Think about the steps and moves you want to make, but don't look down at your feet to do them."

If only she hadn't looked down. Nancy could feel the ropes tangling around her ankles, and when Tanya attempted to lock arms to perform the flip, she couldn't get her feet off the ground. Why she had forgotten something so simple was baffling. In one swift moment, their chance of being named number one in the Freestyle Fusion Double Dutch division of the competition was gone. The audience applauded their performance, but the girls quietly picked up their ropes and walked off the stage.

Tanya stood in total silence as she watched the girls from Jumping Thunder receive the trophy they wanted. Each member on the team also got a beautiful satin jacket. Written across the back of each jacket were the words "Best of the Show." The Double Dutch Club team members each were awarded certificates of participation and red ribbons. All of the participants in the competition had their pictures taken and shook hands with the judges and officials.

Nancy couldn't believe what had happened. She wouldn't bring herself to look directly at any of her teammates. She blamed herself for the loss and didn't know what to say.

Tanya was clearly mad about their team losing. "Why'd you look down? You know you're never supposed to do that!"

Before Nancy could answer, Carla pointed at Nancy's right sneaker. "Look! Nancy's shoelace came apart! She had to stop or you both could have gotten hurt."

"Shoulda kept going," Tanya mumbled and walked to the other side of the backstage area where they had practiced earlier.

Nancy stepped forward and faced her teammates. "I am very sorry for making us lose."

"You did the right thing, Nancy," Coach Hughes said reassuringly. "You *all* did an exceptional job your first time out. I'm proud and I'm pleased with *both* of the performances you gave today."

Nancy sadly looked over to the other side of the waiting area where Tanya was standing against the wall. "I wish Tanya felt the same way."

"I'm sure she'll be fine," said Mrs. A.J. "She just needs a little time for the hurt she's feeling right now to go away. We have a long ride home ahead of us. Let's get our things and head out to the van."

Mr. A.J. carried Ming to the van because the doctor

said she shouldn't walk on her foot. He said she would have to use crutches until her ankle healed.

As everyone gathered her things, Coach Hughes walked over to where Tanya was standing. "You did really good out there today—both times."

Tanya's head was bowed, and she didn't bother to look up. "We shoulda won."

Coach Hughes could see that the toughest girl on the team was crying. She gently touched her on the shoulder. "You did win. You just haven't realized it yet."

Tanya lifted her head and stared at the coach. "That trophy and the jackets—"

"The time will come when you girls are going to win so many trophies and jackets. I have no doubt about that. But I think you were here this time for another reason."

"Another reason like what?"

"Maybe to learn about working together and helping each other out. Remember at one of our earlier practices how you girls helped the others who had fallen?"

Tanya managed to allow a smile to peek through her tears and nodded her head yes.

"That," said Coach Hughes, "was teamwork. There will be many more competitions to look forward to, but today was a special moment for the Double Dutch Club of Grover Cleveland Elementary. I'm sure Nancy and the others wanted to win as much as you did. When

Ming got hurt, our team could have forfeited and given up, but instead, I saw a group of girls who pulled together to make use of what little time they had to practice. I even saw you girls adjust your routine so you could go on. I think that's pretty extraordinary."

Tanya folded her hands and tapped her foot. "I think so too."

Coach Hughes and Tanya walked behind the A.J.s and Mr. and Mrs. Carter and the rest of the team as they headed to the van. All along the way, they received countless hugs, pats on the back, and congratulations from everyone who had come to encourage them. When the girls got inside the van, everyone was silent. Tanya could see Nancy sitting alone in the last seat, looking sadly out the window, so she took the seat next to her. "You jumped good today. Bet if your shoestring hadn't come loose, we woulda showed 'em."

Nancy was surprised at Tanya's compliment. "Thank you. I wish I might have been better."

"It's okay—there's gonna be more jump rope competitions. And we'll win."

"You think so?"

"Girl, I know so!"

On the long ride home, all of the girls had fallen asleep except Nancy. She thought of all that had happened that day. Her team would not be bringing home the grand trophy, but on the inside she felt as if she'd won something even better.

When the girls arrived at school on Monday, they couldn't believe the fuss that was made by their principal, Mr. Redshaw, Mrs. Richards their teacher, and classmates. Coach Hughes, Mr. and Mrs. A.J., the Carters, and family members of all the jumpers came. It was a big surprise. Outside the school hung the banner that Rachel's parents had held during the competition. A reporter and a photographer from the local newspaper also showed up to ask questions and take pictures of the girls and Coach Hughes standing beneath the banner. It had to be the best Monday any of them had ever remembered in the history of Grover Cleveland Elementary.

By the time recess came, everything was pretty much back to normal. There were the kids who sat and talked, some who teamed up for a quick game of football, others who played on the swings, and the Double Dutch Club who jumped on the blacktop.

Ming, who walked on crutches, shouted, "I'll go first!"

"Not today," Rachel responded jokingly. "But soon!"

Nancy and Lindsey started to turn the ropes. "You ready, Carla?" Lindsey asked.

"Bring it!" Carla started to rock a little to match her timing with the turning ropes.

"I'll come in after you!" Tanya shouted.

Suddenly, through the corner of her eye, Nancy thought she saw something moving behind the enormous oak tree. She continued turning, but once again found herself glancing near the tree. Someone was peeking from behind it. Just as Carla entered the ropes, Nancy stopped turning.

"What's going on?" Carla screamed.

Ming called out to Nancy. "Is everything okay?"

Nancy didn't answer anyone. She unraveled the ropes from around her wrists and placed them on the ground. Walking quietly in the direction of the tree, she could hear something. When she stepped behind the tree, there standing alone was a chubby little girl who Nancy thought was about eight or nine years old. "What is your name?" asked Nancy.

Almost in a hush, the girl answered her. "Amber . . . my name is Amber."

"It is a nice name," Nancy told her. She instantly smiled at Nancy. "Are you new here?"

Amber nodded yes.

"Would you like to jump Double Dutch?"

Amber's deep brown eyes lit up with excitement. "Can I?"

"Come with me," Nancy told her.

Amber came running from behind the tree and walked with Nancy to where the girls had continued jumping. "This is Amber," she said, pointing at her. "And she wants to jump Double Dutch."

"Just remember one thing," Tanya shouted.

"Yes, I know." Nancy looked directly at Amber. "You see, Amber, if you want to jump Double Dutch, you must first learn to turn."

"That's right!" Carla chimed.

Rachel, who had been turning, handed the ropes to Nancy. She gently wrapped each one around Amber's wrists, and placed her hands on top of Amber's. She nodded for Lindsey to begin turning the ropes in slow motion. As soon as she felt Amber was getting the knack of it, they sped up the pace. Amber smiled as Tanya, Rachel, and Carla jumped in and out of the ropes while Ming cheered. Nancy loosened her grip of Amber's hands. She was turning the ropes on her own.

Nancy took a glimpse at the beautiful blue sky above her. She realized there had been no mystery to entering the ropes. Once inside, whatever happened was different for each jumper. But one thing they shared was joy. They never actually talked about what made them feel so good, but the smiles and the laughter that took place were common to each of them. Nancy knew it was a special place to be, and she was pleased with what she had found. For just as Constance Howell had written, she had discovered something more precious than gems. Inside the Double Dutch ropes Nancy Adjei had found friends.

As she walked toward the school, a light breeze brushed softly against her cheek and landed like a gentle kiss. Suddenly, she could hear the loving words of her mother reminding her, "God will take care of you." Looking up, her eyes searched far above and beyond the clouds. Quietly she whispered, "That He has done, Mama."

Acknowledgments

This book, *Just Jump*, was conceived in my heart many years ago, and writing it has been a great pleasure. From childhood, I have always been fascinated with the artistic form of rope jumping called Double Dutch. The more I thought about it, the stronger my desire became to share this story about a special time that occurs in the lives of so many young girls. It is a time when the most important thing in the world is getting a chance to "jump inside the turning ropes."

Charles V., thank you for your continuous love and support. You're so inspiring to me.

I give special thanks to "Nina" because she never told me I couldn't.

Janet, Al, and Greg, thank you for your excitement.

Vanessa, thank you for listening to my ideas and liking them.

Cynthia, your enthusiasm helped a few short chapters grow into a beautiful book. Many thanks!

In memory of Ms. Edith Mayner, my mentor, and a "Master Teacher" who refused to accept anything less than the best from all of her students.

And most of all, thank you Lord, for allowing me the opportunity to write for You.

The Negro National Anthem

Lift every voice and sing
Till earth and heaven ring,
Ring with the harmonies of Liberty;
Let our rejoicing rise
High as the listening skies,
Let it resound loud as the rolling sea.
Sing a song full of the faith that the dark past has taught us,
Sing a song full of the hope that the present has brought us,
Facing the rising sun of our new day begun
Let us march on till victory is won.

So begins the Black National Anthem, written by James Weldon Johnson in 1900. Lift Every Voice is the name of the joint imprint of The Institute for Black Family Development and Moody Publishers.

Our vision is to advance the cause of Christ through publishing African-American Christians who educate, edify, and disciple Christians in the church community through quality books written for African Americans.

Since 1988, the Institute for Black Family Development, a 501(c)(3) non-profit Christian organization, has been providing training and technical assistance for churches and Christian organizations. The Institute for Black Family Development's goal is to become a premier trainer in leadership development, management, and strategic planning for pastors, ministers, volunteers, executives, and key staff members of churches and Christian organizations. To learn more about The Institute for Black Family Development, write us at:

The Institute for Black Family Development
15151 Faust
Detroit, Michigan 48223

We hope you enjoy this book from Moody Publishers. Our goal is to provide high-quality, thought-provoking books and products that connect truth to your real needs and challenges. For more information on other books and products written and produced from a biblical perspective, go to www. moodypublishers.com or write to:

Moody Publishers/LEV
820 N. LaSalle Blvd.
Chicago, Illinois 60610
www.moodypublishers.com

ISBN-13: 978-0-8024-2252-1
ISBN-10: 0-8024-2252-7

In the sequel to *Just Jump*, the girls from Grover Elementary return for the new school year only to learn that Ming, their wise leader, has returned to China with her family. They'll have to find someone else to jump Double Dutch with them in time for the December Jump Off. Meanwhile, tough Tanya keeps bumping heads with a new student, Brittany, and is surprised to find the new girl can stand her ground in a fight. Join the adventure in book two of *The Double Dutch Club Series*.

by Mabel Singletary

Available soon at your favorite local or online bookstore.

www.LiftEveryVoiceBooks.com

THE CARMEN BROWNE SERIES

Growing up in a family of five, energetic and confident, Carmen Browne is determined to live her life to please God. Carmen faces some big life issues: an unexpected family move, her big brother's search for his birth family, the tragedy of domestic violence, and her mom's bout with cancer. As she learns to trust God to work all things out for good, Carmen learns a lot about herself, too, especially as she begins to face the uncharted waters of adolescence.

True Friends	0-8024-8172-8	978-0-8024-8172-6
Sweet Honesty	0-8024-8168-X	978-0-8024-8168-9
Golden Spirit	0-8024-8169-8	978-0-8024-8169-6
Perfect Joy	0-8024-8170-1	978-0-8024-8170-2
Happy Princess	0-8024-8171-X	978-0-8024-8171-9

by Stephanie Perry Moore

Find it now at your favorite local or online bookstore.

www.LiftEveryVoiceBooks.com

THE PAYTON SKKY SERIES

The Payton Skky series tells of the spiritual struggles and temptations of Christian high school student Payton Skky. Facing issues such as sexuality, alcohol and drugs, unsaved friends, depression, and the trials of dating puts Payton's faith to the test.

Staying Pure
0-8024-4236-6   978-0-8024-4236-9

Sober Faith
0-8024-4237-4   978-0-8024-4237-6

Saved Race
0-8024-4238-2   978-0-8024-4238-3

Sweetest Gift
0-8024-4239-0   978-0-8024-4239-0

Surrendered Heart
0-8024-4240-4   978-0-8024-4240-6

by Stephanie Perry Moore
Find it now at your favorite local or online bookstore.

www.LiftEveryVoiceBooks.com